FORSAKEN MATE

Vasilisa Drake

CONTENTS

To anyone who has been scared of something and done it anyway.

FANG PACK LAND
HUNTING GROUNDS
ALPHA MANSION
DINING HALL
PACK SCHOOL
TRAINING RING
MAIN STREET
PACK HOUSING
PACK SHOPS
WIND BLOOD PARK LAND
MOON GHOST PACK LANDS

CHAPTER I

I'D BEEN LOOKING FORWARD to today for over a decade.

Tonight, specifically. Tonight was the Choosing.

A strange name, since there was no choice, only the hand of fate to push you forward. A day wolf shifters in all packs looked forward to. Though few perhaps for the reason I did.

But first I had to get through the day. You'd think that today being "The Most Important Day of Our Lives as Young Shifters" (according to my mother, pack elders, teachers, and anyone else who discussed the Choosing) they'd give us the day off from school. Heck, even a half day.

But no. It was our last day as youthful pups, so I was currently enduring sixth period lit like any other day. At twenty years old, as a human, I would've at least had the freedom to skip class in college. The Moon-Ghost pack didn't work like that, so instead, we were treated to an extended period of high school.

It was hard to give a damn. After tonight, I prayed there would be no need for me to return to our pack classes.

I counted down the hours. The ceremony would take place under the light of the full moon when it reached its apex at nearly midnight. It would be about three hours's travel to get there, the pack leaving at nine to converge with two neighboring packs. It was rare, but fated mates were sometimes found in other packs. Better to have that sorted out immediately than deal with soul-torn, star-crossed lovers.

Maddox, our alpha, had made it clear at the last pack meeting that no shameful behavior would be tolerated at the Choosing. No weakness could be shown to our enemies, even if we weren't at war.

I'd learned early on not to show weakness. My enemies were never far.

"I bet her fated mate is a skunk," one of the bitches—it's not sexist if it's literal, right?—was saying behind me. Sabine.

Never mind the fact we all had super hearing.

The male next to her laughed. The teacher ignored it. I tried to as well.

"Better anything than one of the males here," I snapped under my breath. It didn't matter that I was quiet—they heard me. Usually, I could resist responding. It only made it worse for me to provoke them, but what difference would it make today?

Sabine's snarl was a lot louder, earning a growl from the teacher.

She grew silent, but I didn't doubt she was seething. The

Alpha ruled the pack with iron teeth, and no matter how much time she spent cuddling up to the alpha's son, Jett, disrespect for pack elders wouldn't be tolerated by juveniles.

But that would change tonight.

I would find my mate tonight. I refused to consider otherwise. If my mate was in another pack, I'd join before the moon set. With all the cruelty in this world, that was the single kindness: fated mates were respected and never separated.

I'd be lying to say I understood every aspect of the mysticism.

Maybe I'd understand it better if I'd ever seen the love between fated mates up close. But I hadn't. My mother never found her mate. Because of that, how I came to be was a sordid secret. Something my packmates had thoroughly enjoyed speculating about.

It didn't matter. All I cared about was getting out of Moon-Ghost. I refused to believe fate would ever be cruel enough to tie me to someone from this pack.

There's no running away from your pack. You're born in it, you die in it—die for it sometimes too.

"No one in this pack would take her, anyway," Sabine mused when the teacher stepped out of the room for a moment.

"Just like her mother," the male next to her said with a chuckle. Jett.

Sabine was a petty threat. I could've withstood her taunts,

maybe, but when Jett joined in as the alpha's son—and likely the next Alpha of Moon-Ghost—it let everyone else know it was open season on me.

I snarled, my self-control utterly frayed when it came to my mother.

"Oh, don't worry," Sabine said sweetly. "I doubt you'll even be able to keep up. You'll probably stumble on a stone, your pretty red blood running over that disgusting fur until some animal eats you for dinner."

There it was. The real reason I was less than nothing to my packmates.

I kept my eyes pinned on the whiteboard at the front of the room. The two kept trying to provoke me, growing bolder while the teacher was out of the room.

Freak. Defective. Shameful. Failure. Glorified roadkill.

I could've perhaps survived the indignity of my shameful birth if I'd been strong, if I'd blended in with the pack.

I stood no chance at blending in. Wolf shifters came in strict monochromatic colors—dark coal, mottled gray, even the shining white of the Alpha line.

When I shifted, the dark auburn of my hair was preserved in my fur. Normally, physical traits like that had no bearing on our wolf forms. You'd think packmates could look past that, but not in Moon-Ghost.

So that was two marks against me. But the final damning thing?

I was weak.

I was probably the weakest wolf in existence.

If I'd been strong and fast, maybe I could've made up for all my defects, but I struggled. Being in wolf form should've been utterly natural, the purest release of my spirit. Instead, it was painful. Shifting back to human form was involuntary. I was like a child who couldn't control her shift.

No two ways about it: I was the pack freak.

And they never let me forget it. Not for one goddamn day.

The teacher eventually returned, halting the taunts for a bit. The bell rang, ending the day. I quickly gathered my books, determined to escape the school before any of the others could leave the classroom.

"Watch your back, Omega," a voice called after me as I fled.

CHAPTER II

T HE LIVING ROOM WAS immaculate. It always was, not a pillow out of place. It was every room after it that was a disaster. My mother, of course, was not home.

Some things are consistent. Sabine was a bitch. My mother was nowhere to be found.

I glanced inside the fridge. A three-quarters empty bottle of orange juice dangerously close to expiration stared back.

Ugh.

The hours after school before heading to the Choosing should've been exciting. A chance to primp and preen with friends, a chance for family to celebrate the transition from youth to maturity.

Daphne would be with her family now. She'd invited me to join her family for a home-cooked dinner and whatever else loving parents did with their children. I'd declined, less because I had more compelling plans—I obviously didn't—but because I didn't want to make things worse for her.

Her father was the pack's Beta. Theoretically, Daphne should've been guaranteed a spot within the Alpha clique.

Instead, she'd become my best—and only—friend ever since she'd found me stuffed in her locker on the first day of middle school.

Her parents loved her, but they certainly didn't approve. Associating with the pack punching bag was barely tolerated. I felt no need to rub their noses in it.

Instead, I'd meet up with her in six hours, just before we left for the Choosing.

I shut the door on the fridge and went up to my room. I hadn't slept well in weeks. Was it anticipation? Maybe. More like anxiety. I felt frayed at all edges.

And I always looked forward to my dreams.

I settled atop my sheets and shut my eyes. It didn't take long for me to drift off.

"You're back awfully quickly," the voice said in my dream.

The tension eased out of me the instant I heard that voice. My lips curled into a smile while I scanned my surroundings. I was in a beautiful, grassy field with a lake of magma just a dozen steps from my feet. These dreams were always delightfully impossible. I never considered myself a particularly creative person, but my dreams belied that belief.

Dreams were always odd, my imagination conjuring strange places, unlike the simple forests of pack land. Every time I fell asleep, I woke up somewhere completely different.

My imagination also conjured up an imaginary person—who I never saw—for me to talk to.

I'd never confided in Daphne just how powerless I felt in Moon-Ghost. Instead, I kept the thoughts to myself, only giving them brief life while I dreamt.

"I needed to recharge before the big night." I strolled the perimeter of the lava lake, tempted to dive in.

"Of course." The voice sounded vaguely disinterested. "Do you believe you're ready to be mated?"

I knelt down on the edge of the lava and slowly extended a leg, dipping my toe in. The dream lava felt pleasantly warm.

"I want to be free." There was a note of longing in my voice I couldn't hide, but I never hid anything in these dreams anyway. "The only way out of this pack is to mate someone in one of the neighboring packs."

I drew small circles in the lava with my foot. "It wouldn't hurt if my mate is good-looking," I mused. "Even if he's not, I'm sure the moon will take care of the rest."

Moon-matched mates were inevitably drawn to each other. There was, pardon the term, an instant, animalistic attraction.

"So eager for your imaginary mate." The words were dripped in ice. The voice was only my subconscious, of course, but it almost sounded jealous.

It was funny, but whenever my dream conversations turned to matehood these past weeks, that same jealous tone returned. It made me smile.

"Oh, you bet. I'm sure I won't be able to keep my hands off my mate. Considering no one in this pack would lower themselves

to touch me, I'll have a lot to catch up on," I teased.

There was once again an uncomfortable truth in that. I was a wolf shifter. A pack animal. The constant rejection stung, even if I'd long ago learned to toughen my skin to the disdain of those who should've cared for me.

Even if my packmates would've had me, I'd learned my lesson and sworn off them. No, that had been an almost-mistake a few years ago. Fool me once and all that.

"What if you're fated to someone in your pack?" the voice asked, naming my worst fear.

"Fate wouldn't be so cruel." I tried to sound confident as I said it.

"Hmm."

I could taste the skepticism in the air. My gut clenched in fear.

There were only two ways out of the Moon-Ghost pack. Mating a wolf in another pack… and death. Because if anyone tried to escape, the pack enforcers would hunt them to the ends of the world and kill them.

Even if you managed to evade the enforcers for a time, you were marked. At least, that was what the pack elders whispered. Running away was the ultimate sign of disloyalty. No pack would accept you after that. You'd be shunned by the entire world.

I wanted to shrug off the way that terrified me, but that fear was built into my very DNA. Even if I knew Moon-Ghost *didn't deserve a shred of my loyalty, betraying them was un-thinkable.*

No. My mate had to be in another pack, and if the moon had any mercy, I'd meet him tonight.

The voice must've read my thoughts.

"And if you aren't mated tonight?" There was no guarantee, after all.

"I will be." I had to be. "I'm gonna meet my mate tonight, and then everything will be okay."

The voice might've said something more, but suddenly I jolted awake.

Chapter III

M{\small Y EYES FLICKERED OPEN}, and I scanned the room, unmoving in bed. Nothing was out of place in my room. What woke me up?

There. A rustle outside the window.

My hearing wasn't as sharp as most shifters. It was sharper than a human's, but most of my senses were dull in comparison. Still, the rustle was all I needed to shake off the last dredges of sleep.

I didn't move. Not immediately. No, if I made a noise, they'd know I knew they were there. I had to be smart.

My window was open. I kept it locked shut at night, but since it was the afternoon, a boiling day despite the fact we were well into September, I'd risked it open for a breeze.

Stupid. Stupid, stupid, stupid.

Still, the cracked window meant I could hear the voices outside. The rustling grew closer. They were careless.

"Is it even worth it?" one voice whined.

"Shut up." A growl I recognized instantly. Sabine. "It's worth it if I say it is."

The voices were hushed, but I caught the menace in the words easily. I didn't have long. From the sound of it, they were outside my window, planning to climb the tree. For what, I wasn't sure. But I didn't think they'd stop at making funny faces in the window.

Four steps. That was all it would take to get to my bedroom door. From there, I could get out. Not from the front door. Too easy. No, I needed to make sure I'd be harder to reach.

I shifted my weight slowly, rolling onto one side and pressing my leg under me, careful to avoid the noisy springs of my mattress. Omegas didn't get the comfiest beds, but with any luck, this would be the last time I was in it.

"She's gonna pay this time." Sabine's voice floated through the cracked window. They must really think nothing of my hearing abilities.

A part of me wanted to howl. Pay for what imagined crime? What had I ever done to them?

My chest hurt because I knew what my crime was.

I was weak.

They'd picked me out early on, and I'd never been able to fight back. Not in a way that would make them respect me.

But damn if I was going to spend my last day in this pack a punching bag. Confident I'd positioned myself well, I raised myself onto hunched legs, a hand balancing on the edge of the mattress for balance. Then I threw myself across the room. Three strides, but there was no way to dampen the sound.

They'd know I was awake, and Sabine wouldn't give up on her opportunity to torment me that easily.

A snarl confirmed it half a heartbeat later.

I forced myself to ignore it. I ran clear across to the other side of the house and up the stairs to the attic. There was a small window there, sealed shut. I kicked it open, not caring about the consequences.

I pushed my body through, ignoring the distance to the ground. My hand gripped the edge of the roof and I moved my other next to it, hauling myself up.

There. I was on my roof now, which was mostly flat. I walked around to the side where my bedroom was, and there they were. Two of Sabine's crew still in the tree. They were dressed already in the traditional mating-night outfits. It was like prom, in a way. Fancy dresses, beautiful makeup and hair, without a care that it would all be ripped to shreds when we shifted. Or maybe a wedding dress would be a more fitting analogy.

"Glad you all wanted to look your best to see me," I said, fighting to keep my voice steady, confident. Never let them smell your fear, Daphne had told me more than once. I always failed. I was always afraid. But for once, I felt like I could stand up to them. "I really appreciate you taking all that time away from staring at yourself in the mirror to pop by."

Sabine's head poked out my bedroom window. Her perfectly manicured brows were drawn together in anger, and she growled at me. "Get down from there."

Fat chance. I shook my head. "And you asked so sweetly too."

I'd never noticed before, but Sabine had a vein in her forehead that apparently throbbed when she got really angry. Bully for me.

"You're going to regret this." The words were menacing, but for once, they didn't seize me with fear.

"Regret what? Not letting you beat me up? I don't think so," I snapped.

"You'll never be one of us," she hissed.

"Wouldn't want to be," I shot back. I was brave from a distance. And I intended to keep that distance going.

I turned on my heel and started sprinting, her words ricocheting through my head.

You'll never be one of us.

It shouldn't hurt. Not after all these years. They were a bunch of jerks.

But it did. Because deep down, I wanted to belong. I wanted people I would fight for. People I could laugh with. People I could love fiercely.

I didn't let myself dream that my mate would be anything more than my ticket out of this moon-forsaken pack, but in the deepest, most buried part of me, there was the desire.

I wasn't the fastest, but I'd managed to get a head start. Hopefully, that would be enough. I ran as quietly as I could, trying to shield the sound of my steps. The last thing I needed was to get yelled at by the elders.

They weren't as bad as the shifters my own age, but I was an Omega. Always weaker. Always lower in the hierarchy. Always at fault.

I stepped on a familiar roof. Dark gray tile and a brick chimney I could hide behind. I sank down and caught my breath, straining my sub-par hearing for any sound of Sabine.

There was chatter below, and voices inside, but no sign of Sabine and her cronies. Not that I'd expected them to. Sabine might enjoy clawing my face, but she wouldn't want to break a nail of her freshly manicured hand doing it.

Everyone was getting ready. It didn't matter that we'd all be shedding our human skin and shifting when the moon reached its apex.

Inside the house, Daphne was getting ready with her parents. I'd helped her pick out her dress. Her mother was cooing over how beautiful she was and what a powerful mate she'd attract. I doubted the moon cared one way or the other how perfect your eyeliner was, but that was just jealousy. An ugly pang of emotion.

Because where was my mother? I hadn't expected her to shell out money for a dress. But even a few words of encouragement.

Or a goodbye.

But that wasn't our relationship. She'd given birth to me

and, in the most minimal way, took care of me until I could fend for myself. She would never be the type to dote.

Never be the type to love me.

I shook my head. That was old news, a wound that should've healed, but instead, it was like a scab I kept picking at. That wouldn't help anyone.

The only person I cared about was Daphne. I debated giving in to the selfish urge to drop down from the roof and go inside. She'd welcome me with open arms, and she'd be happy I was there.

But her parents wouldn't. And didn't she deserve to have a magical night, with all the pampering and doting that went with it?

So I didn't do that. Instead, I leaned against the chimney, resigned to spending the next hour or two quietly on the roof. I shut my eyes for some semblance of rest, not that I'd let my guard down enough to truly sleep.

CHAPTER IV

"Y ou could've just knocked," Daphne said for the eighth time in half an hour. "Seriously, Avery. The roof?"

I rolled my eyes for the eighth time. "I was trying to be a considerate friend." Daphne frowned. I didn't want to hear it for a ninth time, so I changed the subject. "How much longer do you think it'll be?"

We were riding in Daphne's Jeep. Normally, people just shifted and ran for the night of the full moon, but tonight was different. We were going to meet with two other packs at the mutual edge of our territories. There, under the moonlight, people would find their chosen mates, either in Moon-Ghost or one of the other two—Wind-Blood and the Fangs.

There was no guarantee you'd find your mate. Some of the less lucky wolves in the packs would come back year after year. Others would petition the alpha, Maddox, to find their mate elsewhere.

Maddox always said no. If you went too many years without meeting your moon-matched, tough. Mate with some other luckless bastard. Or Maddox might pair you up himself.

I shivered at the thought. I might be willing to accept the will of our moon goddess—provided it got me out of this pack—but Maddox was no all-knowing goddess.

"Almost there," Daphne assured me.

That was her thing. She was always self-assured. When I asked her if she thought she'd meet her moon-match tonight, she just smiled wistfully and said, "Whatever the moon wills." From anyone else, I'd have scoffed. But that was Daphne. She trusted the process. She didn't have to say it, but I knew she was hoping her mate would be in our pack. Why wouldn't she? Her family had been in the pack since its founding. If not for her friendship with me, she'd be part of the Alpha circle. However much I mocked it, I couldn't deny there were benefits. Acceptance, for one. Power. No one would doubt you belonged.

"You'll meet your mate tonight," she said, offering a kind smile. "You're gonna fall in love and run through the woods and make lots of pups and they're all gonna call me Aunt Daphne and I'll give them candy when you're not looking."

Ninth eye roll of the drive, but I cracked a smile. "You're jumping the gun a bit. Like, by a few miles. But I hope you're right. About the mate thing," I added. I wasn't sure about Daphne feeding my imaginary kids candy.

My chest ached a little. But that would never happen if I joined another pack. There was no mingling beyond the purposes of moon-matching and the occasional bit of resource trading. I'd never see Daphne again.

I knew she wanted to stay in the pack that raised her, and she knew I wanted to escape the pack that had made my life a living hell. We didn't talk about that, though. In fact, we didn't speak for the rest of the drive.

"Here we are," Daphne announced. You couldn't miss the swarm of haphazardly parked off-road vehicles. No one cared about parking neatly on the night of a full moon, apparently. This was also our first official pack run, or it would've been Daphne's. I wasn't exactly welcome. The way the evening went was the three alphas gathered, said whatever moon-magic words that let us all meet our mates, and then while the newly mated shifters ran off to frolic or whatever, the rest of us ran across our respective territories.

Before now, shifters who weren't of age hung back from the rest of the pack and ran amongst themselves. Or at least most of them. I'd never actually been on a pack run, officially or not. It had been made clear early on that I wasn't welcome. And besides, with my weak wolf, I wouldn't be able to keep up, anyway.

Hopefully my mate doesn't mind an Omega. The thought hadn't even crossed my mind until now, though it seemed like it should've been an obvious thought. I could barely manage to shift. I was scrawny. I'd say I could hope to get by on my looks, but aside from the red hair I'd inherited from my unknown father, I was about as visually exciting as banana yogurt.

While I wallowed in a mix of panic and pity, Daphne actually got out of the car, walked to my side, and swung the door open.

"We've got this," she assured me.

"We do." I hoped I sounded as confident as she did.

We weren't the first to arrive by a long shot. Since this was the first official run of the alpha's son, along with a few other notable wolves, I guessed that made sense.

We wandered through the crowd. Daphne waved to her parents but loyally stayed by my side.

"What's she even doing here?" someone said while we walked past. I wish I could say they had the decency to whisper, but why bother? "It's not like she's even going to get a mate. As if the moon goddess would bother."

The person next to them made a sound of agreement and I let out a frustrated breath.

"Ignore them," Daphne said. "Let's check out the other packs."

I ignored them. I bit down so hard I tasted blood, but that was what I did. I held back even while people insulted me to my face.

At least I'd talked back to Sabine today. That had been a victory, even if my only one in recent memory.

As Daphne suggested, we worked our way through the

crowd to catch a glimpse of the other packs. We weren't the only ones either. I spotted Sabine on the other side of the clearing, eyeing some of the Fangs.

So much for loyalty to Jett, huh? Sabine had been talking for years about how she'd be mated with the alpha's son.

Considering Jett was an asshole too, it seemed like a match made in hell.

Still, this was probably the one area I could empathize with.

"Wow," Daphne breathed. "I think I might actually want to mate with a WindBag."

I barked a laugh. "I don't think your mate will appreciate the nickname."

She waved it off. But there was a reason we were all staring. The Wind-Bloods were famous for their speed. They claimed to be the fastest pack on the continent. But they were also one of the most traditional. While the Moon-Ghosts looked ready for prom—except for me, who was still in the same jeans and faded tee I'd worn to school—the Wind-Bloods figured half their clothing would get torn to shreds or misplaced anyway, so they weren't decked in their finest. In fact, they weren't wearing much at all. And being the fastest pack (not that our Alpha would agree with that title) they were all lean, muscled, and for some reason, really freakin' hot. Oh, and the best part? Rather than wearing nice clothes, they got ready by coating each other's skin in oil so their bronzed skins glistened in the moonlight.

One of them, a dark-haired guy who was easily six foot and muscular enough that scrawny was the last word on your mind, spotted Daphne and me. He flexed slightly, reaching his arms behind his back to oil them in a way that was not at all practical except that it highlighted every single muscle of his chiseled torso.

Then he winked at us. Well, at Daphne.

I dug around in my pocket. "Here," I said, handing her some clean tissues.

She managed to tear her eyes away from the dark-haired shifter long enough to give me a confused look. "What are these for?"

"Your drool," I explained.

Daphne laughed and laughed. Then she winked back at the guy and he actually stumbled.

I was going to miss my best friend.

On the other side, completing the triangle, were the Fangs. Unlike the Moon-Ghosts, who wore their finest, or the Wind-Bloods who wore next to nothing, the Fangs hit an entirely different dress code. They weren't just a pack either. They were a biker gang, and the members dressed the part. Black leather, metal studs that reflected the moonlight. Where we'd used jeeps, they arrived on motorcycles.

I eyed one of the Fangs our age who was nearby. He had pale blond hair and an easy smile as he surveyed the surroundings. Both belayed the dark biker image, but I didn't mind the contrast. I let my attention linger. What was the harm? Everyone was sizing each other up. And between the Wind-Bloods and the Fangs, I thought I might actually prefer the biker gang pack. With my weak wolf, I wouldn't fit in a clan built for athletics. But bikes? I'd love to get on one, even just once. I smiled faintly, thinking of how it would feel. Freeing, I decided. Wind blasting me, nothing in my way. I could go as fast and as far as I damn well pleased.

In my daydream, I'd stopped noticing the blond shifter as anything but a proxy for my freedom fantasies.

"See something you like?" the blond asked, a smirk on his lips that was teasing but lacked the casual cruelty I'd grown used to.

I blinked for a moment, startled that he was speaking to me. "Me?"

Daphne elbowed me before stepping aside in a smooth motion. I stared at her retreating back. *Traitor,* I thought silently.

"You kept staring at me, so I thought you might like a closer look."

"Sorry," I stammered, face flushed.

"Nothing to be sorry about. Can't say I wasn't doing the same thing after all." The smirk didn't leave his face.

Wait. Was he... was he *flirting* with me?

He reached out and fingered a stray lock of my hair. "Do you dye it?"

Speechless, I shook my head. "All natural." His mouth opened, and I cut him a look. "And I'd appreciate skipping any lame questions about the curtains matching the drapes."

"What, you're decorating our house already? Eager, but I can work with that," he teased. "Actually, I was going to say it's stunning. Like liquid fire. And clearly, you've got the attitude to match."

I snorted. Attitude? I had just enough bite to keep me from being devoured entirely. "Thanks." The word made for lousy conversation, but I had no idea how to handle conversations like this. Where a guy actually liked me, that is. There was a beat of silence, and for some anxious reason, I asked, "Is this your first time?"

"Second, actually. But you could say I'm feeling lucky this year." He pushed another lock of hair behind my ear.

It was a sweet gesture. I kind of wanted to shake my hair free because I hated having it tucked behind my ears like that, but I resisted. Instead, I smiled. "Me too," I agreed. "Well, feeling lucky. It's my first time."

"I figured," he said, utter smoothness. "I'd remember you." Corny, but I was smiling anyway. There was a howl, and then others joined in. Showtime. "I'll see you around," the blond biker promised, and I mumbled, "See you," like I wasn't secretly hoping I'd just met my mate.

Get a grip! I didn't even know his name, and he'd already rejoined his pack by the time I realized I should've asked.

But there it was. That stupid spark of hope that never went out. The one I nurtured in those dream conversations, where I imagined a world where I had my moon-matched mate. Where I wasn't hated. Where I was free.

CHAPTER V

I SHOOK MY HEAD and rejoined the Moon-Ghosts, ignoring the side eyes as I settled next to Daphne. People were still talking and mingling as we circled around. It was a rare chance to see the other packs, and that always made for good gossip, even if we'd only been around for an hour. Long enough that the sun had fully set, the moon high in the sky.

In the center of the field was a rock formation. Moon rock, because everything sacred was named after the moon. The three alphas stood on it, rising above the crowd. I spotted the alpha's son, Jett, along with the Alpha clique—Sabine and the rest—towards the front. Well, just as well for me to be in the back, even though Daphne kept trying to elbow us forward.

"Welcome, shifters." Maddox's voice rang out. Even though the packs were supposed to be gathered as equals, Maddox had edged an inch in front of the others and was the first to speak. Our Alpha didn't enjoy sharing the spotlight. "It is our most sacred night, the night where the Moon Goddess may deign to bless the most worthy of us, strengthening our packs as she sees fit." He seemed to manage eye contact with every single person in the crowd before settling his attention in front of him.

Of course, Maddox would focus on strength. There was no doubt in my mind I didn't meet his definition of worthy, either. But his son, who practically preened, did. A prince among us peasants.

"And more importantly," another alpha—the Wind-Blood one, from the looks of it—cut in smoothly, "as we all most desire, may she bless each one of you with your moon-matched mate." There were some cheers after that, and Maddox looked a bit sour. No one had cheered at his coldhearted statement.

The third alpha, from the Fangs, grinned at us. It was a wicked showing of teeth. "And barring all that, let's run like the blazes under the full moon the way we were born to."

At that, more cheers erupted. As much as we all hoped to meet our fated mate, it wasn't strictly realistic. An awesome run was more attainable.

But I would. I could feel it in my blood, with a comforting certainty. I would meet him, and he would take me away from everything rotten in my pack.

"For whatever reason the goddess wishes, we're all gathered under one moon tonight." Maddox's words rang through the crowd. "And as my son has come of age, he shall be given a special honor. If the moon wills it, he will meet his mate tonight." He held out a hand grandly in front of him. "Join us, son of mine and future Alpha of the Moon-Ghost pack."

The other alphas didn't look thrilled, but they didn't object. Jett didn't need a second invitation, joining his father on the rock in a single leap.

In that moment, with the moonlight beaming down on him, he looked every bit the Alpha prince. His long, black locks shone in the moonlight, his suit clearly tailored to fit his muscled body. He wasn't as bulky as his father, but he would grow into a large, brutal frame. That I didn't doubt. But for now, he looked like all he was missing was a crown.

"Moon Goddess!" Maddox called out.

The other alphas repeated the words, then the crowd took up the cry.

"Moon Goddess! Moon Goddess! Moon Goddess!" Even Daphne joined in the chant, but I couldn't do more than stare.

The night seemed to grow brighter, like the moon was shining more brightly. It was... unnerving. Of course I believed in the Moon Goddess. But I'd never seen her called on and answered.

Maddox cut off the chants with a wave of his hand and a silence fell over us.

"Moon Goddess, I ask you: bless my son, Jett King, and if his fated mate is here tonight, I beseech you to show us his moon-match." He said the word beseech, but it sounded more like a command.

But then... then the moon answered. The light grew brighter, but it seemed to gather only on Jett. It was like he was the Moon Goddess's favorite, and she was letting us know. He was a silver prince. Everyone's attention was fixed on him, and he knew it. You could feel every female shifter in the crowd praying they'd be chosen as his mate. The Alpha prince's expression turned domineering. He surveyed us as if we were all his subjects. Still, there was something almost magnetic. I'd never been one for Jett's charms, but tonight, he was the most handsome man I'd ever seen. Somehow, I forgot every cruel thing he'd ever done to me, every taunt, every beating. They meant nothing if I could just keep looking.

I took a step forward, not even realizing it. How was everyone else just standing still? He was an angel. He was beautiful. Another step. Closer. I had to be closer.

"No."

The word barely penetrated the haze of desire. I wanted to get closer, to tear off that suit with the claws that hid beneath my human skin. And maybe I was imagining it, but Jett seemed to be looking at me too. His wild gaze was intoxicating. My blood warmed with want. Raw want.

"This cannot be. I won't allow it!" A snarl, and years of being an Omega made me hesitate when I heard that tone. Because that was the sound of a very, very angry Alpha and it was loud enough to make me freeze.

My view of Jett was blocked, and I almost growled despite

myself. His father stepped in front, and he seemed to be looking at me.

"Avery..." My best friend breathed my name no louder than a whisper. "You're his mate."

"What? No," I answered on a reflex, not even looking back at her. I tried to angle to see Jett.

"Look at yourself. The moon chose you." She tugged at my wrist and I glanced down.

My skin was glowing too. A silver brightness, identical to Jett's.

What?

How could this be?

A part of me remembered this was wrong. My mate wasn't supposed to be in Moon-Ghost. Certainly not the alpha's son. Not my tormentor.

Down to my soul, there was a newfound peace wrapped in an ache. If I could just get closer to him. Then everything would be right. There was bone-deep certainty in that. I couldn't understand what it meant, not logically. But my body knew. It rejoiced in the sensation, it craved closeness.

But why wasn't he coming to me? Why was he just standing there, half-hidden by his father? Didn't he feel this? The rightness? The wanting?

My mate—because he was, for better or worse, and at the moment it felt wonderful. Everything would be okay.

But still, my mate didn't move. And I was still frozen in

place.

A heartbeat later, Jett stepped in front of his father. My gaze raked over him as if drinking in the sight like it was the first gulp of air I'd been allowed in my life. Desperately choking it, but grateful for the sight.

There was need in his eyes. I saw it. I knew it matched my own.

But there was another emotion in there, and it was nothing kind. Nothing gentle.

And then he spoke. He didn't raise his voice, not like his father, but the packs were silent. Waiting to hear his next words. The Alpha and the Omega. Mismatched but moon-matched too.

"Avery Ward, the moon goddess has offered you to me. But you're no mate of mine. You're weak. Unworthy. Pathetic. I feel sick looking at you. This is the Choosing, so heed my choice." There was a beat. Just a single pause before the next words left his mouth and destroyed the last glimmer of hope I'd felt.

"I forsake you as my mate."

Chapter VI

Forsaken.

The air disappeared. I couldn't breathe. There was a crushing feeling like my lungs were being squeezed. It was sudden and paralyzing, and then it was gone. And all I was left with was a bone-deep ache and a sense of wrongness that made me want to sob. It was like everything I was, down to my very soul, had been drenched in sludge.

This was the Choosing.

Not just the moon's choice but ours too. But what choice had I been given?

Being forsaken was cruelty beyond belief. The elders rarely spoke of it. It wasn't like a divorce. You didn't yell at each other screaming, "If you're so sick of how I wash the dishes, then forsake me and be done with it!"

Forsaking... didn't happen.

But it had happened to me.

It didn't matter that I detested Jett and everything the pack stood for. That he'd terrified me for years. That I'd never wanted to be tied to someone in this cursed pack. The moon had chosen us, and he'd... he'd forsaken me. There was nothing rational about how I felt. Nothing logical. Just raw instinct driving me.

I did the only thing I could. The only thing I'd ever been able to do.

I ran.

I ran and ran and ran as far as my legs would carry me. I wasn't the fastest or strongest, but no one followed me right away. I reached the woods. Whose territory I was technically in, I didn't know. I didn't care. I collapsed behind a tree and sobbed.

I hadn't even known I could make sounds like that, but once they started, they didn't stop. Tears, even though I never cried, flowed painfully. Time meant nothing. All I felt was this visceral loss. Everything hurt. My chest, lungs, heart, throat. My head ached. I pressed a hand to my forehead. I was boiling. Feverish.

But I was so broken.

I wanted to escape the pack, and maybe I'd still get my wish. Surely they'd let me leave the pack now. Without a mate, though, I had nowhere to go. But wouldn't I be free? A kind of free?

I tried to console myself, but that awful, gripping pain in my chest wouldn't ease. Then, at the edge of my senses, I heard a sound. Not a normal rabbit moving around, but something bigger. A group? I strained my hearing and my blood ran ice-cold.

"She's around here somewhere. I can tell." That voice. My mate's voice.

I shuddered another sob at the sound. How cold. Didn't he feel this? It's not like it was a choice, this moon-matched, moon-cursed thing. Shouldn't he be in pain like I was? Shouldn't it feel like the universe was collapsing on him?

"We'll take care of it. You won't even have to touch her. That bitch is going to regret the day she was born." Sabine. Sounding more feral than I'd ever heard. Whether it was anger, protectiveness, or just raw delight at the thought of punishing me. Like any of this had been my choice.

Survive. No matter how shitty I felt, I had to survive. Those instincts overruled everything, just powerful enough to cut through the fog.

I stood on shaky legs, forcing myself off the forest floor.

"There," someone said. Shit. Their hearing was better than mine, and on the night of the full moon, it was unparalleled.

There would be no subtlety. I ran.

And they chased. I could sense them. I was more prey than predator. Weak. But desperate to live. I ran, but they ran faster. I didn't know where I was. There were no familiar landmarks, no places to hide.

They were gaining on me. I strained, pushing myself harder than I ever had before. Live. I had to live.

Then, pain. Sudden, hot pain erupted across my torso. I

was knocked to the ground, my arms barely breaking my fall. I tried to crawl back, to regain my footing, but Sabine was faster. She pounced and slapped me. Her claws raked across my face. I tasted blood. My ears rang while my mind tried to process what was happening.

"Goddess, that felt good," she hissed. "You're going to die tonight."

My torso burned as I tried to stand. Her fist slammed into me.

"Why?" I coughed out. Part of me was trying to stall, to distract her. But why? Why kill me? Wasn't I already ruined?

Naively, I never thought, as cruel as Sabine had been, that she would be a murderer.

The gleeful, fiendish light in her eyes told me I'd been an idiot.

"You dumb slut." There was a righteous lilt to her words that made me want to tremble. Or maybe that was the blood loss. "You think you can just walk away? Our Alpha can't have a forsaken mate"—even hearing the words felt like a blow—"out in the world, shacking up with anyone who will tolerate you and siring bastards."

I tried to gather my limbs under me while she talked. Behind her was one of the wolves from the Alpha clique.

And Jett.

He stood there. There was hate in his eyes. Nothing tender. No regret. He might not be beating me himself, but he wanted Sabine to kill me. It shouldn't have hurt. He should've meant nothing.

But it all hurt. It hurt so freaking much.

"This is the end for you. I almost pity you, but you can't pity what you hate," she spat. And then she lunged.

I managed to jump back, dodging at the last second.

It wasn't enough, though. Sabine didn't give up like that. She lunged for me again, and this time she made contact.

I couldn't just let her hit me. The pain awakened something inside me, something more desperate than I'd ever known. I wanted to live, dammit. I fought. I fought harder than I'd ever fought for anything. I clawed wildly. The scent of blood filled the air. The scent of death.

But it was my blood.

The pain turned to a dull ache, and I ignored it while I clawed. But there was no end to the assault. If I nicked her, she cracked one of my ribs. If I dodged her, she just came at me harder. I was a cornered animal, lashing out, but she was an apex predator.

Then, a lucky strike. I slashed her eye and she howled in pain. Her roar shook the woods.

I didn't hesitate. I scrambled back, running. But a moment later, the others were on my tail.

Run faster, I willed myself. I was limping, trying to weave through trees. Run. Escape. Recover. If I could escape them, I could find help. Who would help me? I didn't know. A pack healer. Someone. But I had to escape. Get back to the crowd.

And then I reached the edge of the woods.

But it wasn't clear fields on the other side.

It was a cliff.

Shit. Shit, shit, shit.

The others caught up. Sabine's face was covered in blood and a hasty bandage torn from the other shifter's shirt. The only reason I'd made it this far, no doubt.

"Please," I begged. I hated begging, but it was better than death. "You'll never see me again. Just let me go."

"Never."

The word came from Jett. The single time he spoke during this.

"I hate you all!" I screamed. "You're going to kill me, and for what? It's not enough to forsake me?" My words were slurred slightly. The blood loss. I could feel it soaking through my tattered jeans. My shirt was nothing more than an ambitious scrap of cloth, my organs threatening to fall out.

Even if I got to a healer, it might be too late.

"I'll be kind," Jett said.

I barked a hysterical laugh at that. I couldn't help it.

"Kind?" My voice was shrill.

"Jump." He said it like he hadn't heard me speak. "Just step off the cliff and it can all be over."

I stared at him like he was insane. He wanted me to kill myself? Too good to get his own hands dirty? I growled.

"Never." I wasn't sure where the resolve came from. I didn't care.

"To hell with this," Sabine announced.

She rushed me, throwing me back with all her strength.

This was the end.

I wasn't even sure when I hit the ground.

Chapter VII

There was nothing. For a second or forever, I couldn't tell. There was no time, and I had no body. Only nothingness.

But somehow, I was cold.

Chapter VIII

I'D NEVER BEEN SURE if I bought more into the whole traditional Heaven and Hell thing or the pack's belief of our spirits turning into stars. I was definitely leaning toward the former because I wasn't a star.

At least, not unless stars had massive headaches.

I shook myself awake and noticed something was different. Really different.

I was in my wolf form.

For a moment, I just stared at myself in shock. Well, down at my paws, since there wasn't a mirror or anything.

Just like my human hair, my fur was bright red. I normally felt wobbly, off balance in my weaker form.

I took a tentative step forward, and... that wobbliness was gone. Instead, I felt steady on my legs, comfortable, like my fur was a proper second skin. For a moment, there was delight.

But there was still a lingering ache, a sadness. The broken mate bond.

Everything crashed back into me. The ceremony. The attack. The cliff.

Sabine had pushed me. Even if she hadn't, I'd been near dead.

But I wasn't at the base of a cliff. Instead, I was in the middle of a field.

I raised my nose and inhaled the scents. They weren't anything I'd ever scented on Moon-Ghost territory, nor did I recognize where I was. But there was something almost familiar about the scent.

Something tugged at my senses, an awareness that was both my own and yet foreign at the same time. I followed it, taking off in a direction without a care.

I must've been dreaming because I'd always been weak. Unsteady. Slow. Yet here, in my wolf form, I felt anything but. Every step was self-assured, and my body showed no sign of tiring as I ran mile after mile through fields.

It was nighttime. My surroundings were painted in darkness, the moon nowhere to be seen. Only stars lit the way, allowing me to see. My rational, human mind tried to make sense of that. The moon had been full the last time I was awake. Or alive.

But my wolf didn't care.

In our wolf forms, shifters became more animal than human on a deeper level. It was a delicate balance, and not every shifter experienced the same change. Some were more animal in human form than others were in wolf form. The more powerful the shifter, the more balanced they were supposed to be in both forms. But I'd never really experienced the raw, instinctual pull on the rare occasions I'd shifted before.

But now? My wolf was out and she was in control.

She was ruled by instinct, and her instincts commanded her to chase this awareness. It tugged me, drawing me farther and farther. The fields were grass, then covered in flowers. There were orchards, then proper forests. I reached a lake and started to circle the bank, tilting my head as I went, as if it would let me better follow the invisible guiding force.

Then, as suddenly as it had come, it faded.

Once gone, I could think more clearly. Where was I? I still had no clue. I'd been running for hours if I had to guess, but nothing was familiar. I'd never been here before.

And I hadn't seen anyone either.

Could I really be dead?

I mean, there was no way I could've survived the fall. But I didn't feel dead, right? Not that I was an expert in the subject.

Suddenly thirsty, I stepped down to the lake to drink some water. I sniffed the surface, but it smelled... odd. Not wrong, exactly, but not like plain water. My wolf turned her snout up to it and decided to look for another source of water.

Then, a flash of movement. My inner predator woke up, and without another thought, I was chasing it.

How bizarre. How right. For years, I'd been the one on the run. A wolf-shifter, hunted by my own kind. Yet here, I was like any of the others. I was a huntress.

And, well, I was hungry.

I chased down the rabbit and ruthlessly bit in. The human part of me felt bad, but the wolf was simply pleased to have caught something and dealt with the hunger.

What now?

I now knew food could be found in the area, and there was water, even if it turned out my wolf was a water snob. I could always shift and drink that way, even if I'd never heard of the human side needing to outmaneuver the wolf. Normally our wolves had better survival instincts than we did. That left shelter.

I looked around. The area was mostly exposed. There was a wooded area a half-mile back, maybe, but I didn't relish the idea of sleeping in a tree. Especially since I'd need to shift into my human form and I'd be exposed to the elements.

I surveyed the area. There were some mountains in the distance to one side, the lake to the other. Seemed like the woods were my best bet.

I turned back the way I'd come and when I returned to the woods, I took them in properly. I'd have to shift back to human at some point and better examine the area. For now, though, my wolf form was a safer bet. I was faster, stronger. Whether those changes would hold when I shifted back, I couldn't guess. Especially since shifting had never felt like this before.

From my limited view as a wolf, the trees didn't look like

anything that was native to my pack's territory. Without that strange urge to distract me, I could better take in the area. It wasn't entirely deserted like I'd previously thought. There were some rabbits and field mice. That much was normal, at least.

Just when I thought I'd have to settle for a tree after all, I found a cave. There were strange scents clinging to it, but it would have to do. The cave wasn't huge, but it was large enough for me to tuck myself in a decent distance out of sight and stand if I shifted back.

I tucked myself into a corner, setting myself up to keep an eye on the entrance while hidden from sight.

This night had been impossibly long. I'd thought I would find my freedom in my mate, and instead... I'd gotten whatever this was. The broken bond was still like shards of glass in my chest. I hoped it would fade eventually, or I really would wish I was dead.

With that cheerful thought, I let sleep overtake me.

THERE WAS NO FIELD or pond, not like when I normally dreamed. I was human again, but I couldn't see anything. There was only darkness, and strangely, it was more a feeling than something I saw. There was sorrow and pain and a gut-wrenching hurt.

"Where have you been?"

The voice. At least, wherever I was, whatever was happening with my wolf, my subconscious was still keeping up with these dream conversations.

Still, this was different. Normally the voice of my imaginary conversation partner was warm, comforting, if a bit teasing. Now, it was almost angry.

"Is your mate not letting you get any sleep?" the voice demanded.

What? Was my subconscious going to rub in that I'd had the worst mating in the history of matings?

All I could manage was a snort. "Depends on your definition of sleep." He'd certainly tried to put me in a permanent one.

"Jump," he'd said. Like I was an inconvenience, and couldn't I do him this one favor of killing myself?

Bastard.

Yet involuntarily, it hurt. Like a betrayal. Even though I never should've expected anything from Jett.

"What do you mean?" There was still an anger to the words, but it didn't feel directed at me. Tension was tightly corded through his words. "Did he do something to you?"

"You could say that." I felt defeated, just remembering the evening. The darkness wrapped me in a cocoon, the sadness so potent I felt like I was drowning.

"Tell me," the voice ordered.

I didn't know how to. "You sound different," I said, not

wanting to address the events with my subconscious. Wasn't it enough that I lived them?

And the voice did. It was clearer, in a way. But it was probably just my imagination. What else could it be?

"Tell me what happened, Avery. You feel different."

"Well, I think I'm dead." It was supposed to be a joke, but it fell flat as I said it because I just wasn't sure.

There was silence, but there wasn't stillness. Everything shook, violent as an earthquake.

"Avery? Tell me where—" But the voice never got to finish his demand. The darkness was torn away with an abruptness that left me spinning.

And I was looking into two extremely angry, red eyes.

CHAPTER IX

THE FIRST THING I noticed were the eyes. Inches from mine, angry, and on a face that wasn't human. Not even close.

The second thing I noticed was that I was fucked.

The creature towered over me. Which wasn't hard because I was lying on the ground.

In my human form.

I must've shifted in my sleep. I hadn't even known that was a risk. A lifetime without shifting properly left me woefully ill-equipped.

"What are you doing in my cave?" the creature roared.

It was humanoid but monstrous. A bull's head with horns that scraped the top of the cave in a terrible screech. The body of a human. The most grotesque incarnation of one. Dark blue skin stretched over a body that was pure muscle. Easily three hundred pounds of it.

Shit, shit, shit.

"Um. Well. Here's the thing," I stammered, trying to think fast. I stretched back against the wall and stood slowly, trying

not to enrage the beast. I was naked, but the angry creature
didn't give a damn. There was murder in its eyes, not lust. I
wasn't sure it would've been worse. "I was tired and needed
a place to sleep." I tried to see past the monster while I explained.

"This is my cave!" the beast shouted. Spit left its bull snout,
spraying me, and I tried not to recoil.

I couldn't shift. That would take too long. But I'd be
damned if I let the monster cow me.

I straightened, rolling my shoulders back. "I didn't know
that. It's not like there was a sign for me!"

"I marked it! It's mine!"

This time, an angry splatter of spit splashed right across my
cheek. I growled. Okay, so there'd been an odd scent. How
was I supposed to know it belonged to this thing?

Unfortunately, my growling only seemed to infuriate the
monster further.

"Look, I just needed a place to rest. I'll be on my way, and
you'll never see me again." I made a move to pass the monster,
but he slammed me back against the stone wall. His hand had
human fingers, not hooves, but the nails were long and dug
into my shoulder. I hissed. "Not cool!"

The monster roared in response. Apparently, he didn't give
a shit about being cool.

"No one trespasses on me!"

Another vicious smack, but I dodged it. Barely.

The monster reached back, determined to beat my skull in.

No.

Not again.

I was done being a victim.

I shoved back. Pushed with all my strength, my anger. Fury. All my life, people had bullied me. Picked on me. Took their anger out. And what had I ever done to deserve it? I might be in hell, but dammit, I wasn't going to be hell's submissive bitch. I was going to fight.

So when I shoved, I reached deep. I pushed as hard as I could because I wasn't going down without a fight.

The push should've done nothing. The creature had several hundred pounds on me easily. A small stumble would've been gratifying enough to give me hope. I'd follow it with a groin kick and hope the monster's anatomy was close enough to a human male's. Go for the knees. Punch his nose.

But I didn't do any of those things.

Because when I made contact with the blue-tinged flesh, the creature flew back across the cave, its back slamming into the wall with an audible thunk. Green sparks tinged the air, gone so quickly I must've imagined them. The monster's eyes were shut, blood dripping down the cavern walls.

I stared for three seconds. Enough to let my disbelief sink in.

Holy shit. I'd just knocked out a creature three times my size.

The creature's chest was still rising and falling. Not dead. For some reason, probably a lack of self-preservation, that was a relief.

And with that, I sauntered from the cave. No more running for this girl.

I WASN'T SURE HOW long I'd slept for, but it was a day. Or at least, this realm's variant of it. The sky was bright, but instead of the comforting blue hue, it was a pale red.

I was pretty damn sure I wasn't on the continent anymore. At least, not any of the parts I was familiar with. Between the sky, the monster, and the fact I could shift easily, something was seriously screwed up. Maybe a coma-induced dream? I wasn't this creative. And it didn't feel like a dream.

Then again, I didn't feel dead either, and that was my second guess.

Dead or not, I wouldn't find any answers standing around in the woods. I turned what I guessed was west, perpendicular to the direction I'd woken up and the lake I'd run to, and started walking.

The landscape was similar to yesterday, though the realm was different through human eyes. My wolf was guided by raw instinct, joined with scent and keen hearing. As a human, I focused more on what I could see. My wolf had only been able to make out vague mountain peaks in the distance. With human eyes, I took in their true size. Massive. Bigger than any of the ranges that bordered our pack lands.

Well, not my pack lands anymore.

There was still an ache from the mate bond shattering. But I forced myself to ignore it. I wouldn't let them cripple me. I'd survived—well, that was to be determined—everything else they'd thrown at me, every hateful threat or punch. This wouldn't break me.

But goddess, it was hard to ignore.

I tried to gather my thoughts, but that was impossible to do without thinking of yesterday. Of Jett. Of Daphne, my best friend. What was she thinking? It would've been one thing for me to properly leave the pack. That we were prepared for. But this? Everything hurt, a painful jumble of thoughts. I focused on putting one step in front of the other. I needed to find someone I could talk to who wouldn't try to kill me for no reason.

Sadly, if past experience was anything to go by, that was a tall order.

I had no urge to run like yesterday. I walked for most of the day, stopping at a river to drink water. I didn't have my wolf form's affinity for rabbit hunting, so I didn't eat. There were berries on some wild bushes, but they didn't look like anything I'd ever seen. And since I wasn't about to die by eating random poisonous crap, I made myself continue. The sky took on a darker tint, signaling what must've been evening after only a few hours. I'd have to stop soon, and I wasn't keen to try my luck on another cave.

Then, when I crested another in a series of unending hills, I saw it.

A castle. An honest-to-goddess castle, like something out of a medieval documentary. Excited, I increased my pace. It stood alone with no other structure around it. There had to be people there. Help, if I was lucky, or at least answers.

The castle was massive, larger than several houses put together. It had a drawbridge, which was down. I took a step on it and stared at the moat. It wasn't water circling the castle, but lava.

The lava tickled at a memory in the back of my head, but it was just out of reach. Where would I have seen lava anyway? It's not like I'd lived near active volcanoes.

The only way in seemed to be through the front doors, so I crossed the drawbridge without another backward glance. The doors were shut, however. I knocked on them, trying to announce myself. When that didn't work, I banged on the door, hoping the noise would permeate the massive structure.

Instead, my pounding pushed the door open. A loud creak cut through the silent evening.

Unlocked. Weird. But then again, it was weird to have a castle in the middle of nowhere. A castle surrounded by lava. I'd need to recalibrate my assessment of weirdness.

"Hello?" I called, walking inside.

The castle was all stone, unsurprisingly. Black, shiny stone, completely different from the plain gray of the outside. Polished marble or something similar. The walls were covered in tapestries, visible in the light of massive braziers that hung from the ceilings and the torches that dotted the wall.

"Is anybody home?" I called again, wandering deeper.

No answer.

I shivered. Outside could pass for early fall weather, not uncomfortably cold. Inside the castle was downright chilly. I needed to either find some clothes or shift back into a wolf if I didn't want various bits and pieces to start freezing off. Settling on the former, I started to explore the castle. There was no sign of anyone.

That was just as well, given that I was naked, I figured. But I'd need answers sooner than later.

The castle seemed empty but not abandoned. There was no dust, for one. Not a single cobweb.

Each corner was punctuated with a statue. Some looked fairly normal; others, like the monster from this morning. Or worse. Women with claws for hands, winged creatures with inhuman faces. I avoided looking at them. Something about the statues set my teeth on edge.

They're just statues, I chided myself. *Focus.*

I passed by a few rooms, but they were empty or useless. A sitting room with furniture, but no clothing. Another that seemed almost like a gallery with massive paintings lining the wall. Some doors were locked, and I wasn't able to brute force my way through. Apparently, my newfound strength wasn't without limits.

Finally, a bedroom. The door was shut, but when I pushed against it, just like the castle's door, it slid open. The door was silent on the hinges. I crept in on instinct, then shook my head. No one was here. I'd been stomping around the castle for the better part of an hour. If someone was here, surely they'd have confronted me by now.

The room opened to a bed. Promising because bedrooms hopefully meant spare clothing. If nothing else, I could grab a sheet or something. The sheets were already in disarray on the bed, in a hazardous heap rather than neatly made. Odd, since everything else I'd come across was arranged perfectly. But whatever. Maybe I could hunt down whoever slept in this room and ask them some questions.

But first... hopefully they wouldn't mind sharing their clothing.

A massive wardrobe sat opposite the bed, and I beelined for it. I was freezing, after all. I quickly looked through, searching for something warm.

Whoever lived here was bigger than me. There were some folded slacks, but they were about three sizes too big. The shirts were more promising. Still large, but that could work. I slipped on a crisp, white button-down. Surprisingly warm.

The shirt fell to mid-thigh, which was good in case I ever found someone I'd actually need to be modest around.

I searched for other clothes, but the offerings were sparse. I did find a pair of socks tucked away, which would be a blessing while walking around a stone castle.

I bent over to slip them on when there was a rustling sound behind me.

"Comfortable?" a half-asleep voice rumbled.

Chapter X

I SPUN, STARTLED.

The bed, as it turned out, wasn't just covered by a mess of sheets. Someone had been sleeping in there.

Not just someone. A man.

The word felt like an understatement because there were no men who looked like this. His body was still hidden by the sheets, but he'd propped himself up on the headboard, a bicep flexed like a makeshift pillow. Dark hair curling around his ears in an effortless mess that I wanted to run my hands through. A sharp jaw that was softened by the barest hint of stubble over tanned skin. His lips were full, biteable, and curved into what looked like the beginning of a laugh. A laugh where I wasn't in on the joke. My attention shifted up. Long lashes framed his eyes in a way that made their gaze magnetic. He was the most handsome man I'd ever seen, but it wasn't just his physical features. There was something dark about him, not in his features, but in the air around him. How hadn't I sensed him? Now that I saw him, his presence consumed the room.

And the eyes. Those weren't human eyes. Not shifter eyes either. Twin amber orbs that seemed to glow in the dim light. And they were fixed on me.

Those amber eyes flared for just a moment when our gazes met.

"What a strange place for me to find you," he mused.

"I kept calling out," I said defensively. "I don't know how the hell you didn't hear me."

"Voices are strange things," he said neutrally. "Tell me, little wolf, why are you here?"

I frowned at the endearment. "How do you know I'm a wolf?" I demanded. "Who are you?"

Those amber eyes flared again, and then there was a shift. I wasn't sure how to describe it, but there was a change.

"It's rude to question someone in their own home."

He was out of bed in one swift movement. One second he'd been propped under the sheets, the next, those same sheets were torn aside and he was standing in front of the bed, stalking toward me.

It was an effort not to flinch.

He was tall. Probably a foot taller than me. Under those sheets, he'd been shirtless. Now his torso was on full display.

God, he was perfect.

A tattoo stretched around his chest, winding around his back. A pair of black pants hung dangerously low on his hips. His movements out of the bed were unhurried, but they made me want to run.

But not anymore. I was done running. I'd run and run my whole life out of a sense of self-preservation, and where had it gotten me?

The world was frozen for those seconds while he moved towards me. His body seemed to take up the whole room, which made no sense, but I felt it with every fiber of my being. He didn't stop moving until he was a foot from me.

A bolt of pain went through my back. I'd taken a step back.

No. Never again. I forced myself to press off of it, even if it meant there were scant inches between us. He stared down at me, eyes fixed on my every movement. I wanted to growl.

"What are you doing in my home?" he demanded.

"The door was open," I huffed. "If you don't want people walking in, consider investing in a lock."

"That's because the inhabitants of this realm know better to stumble in." His lips parted, but it was less a smile and more a showing of teeth. "If they do, they don't leave. Not in one piece."

I rolled my eyes. "How scary. Very convincing."

Okay, it was a little menacing. Most people blustered when they made threats. They tried hard to sound big and scary and powerful.

The male in front of me sounded more like he was reminiscing.

"But considering you seem to spend your whole day sleeping, I doubt you're anything to be scared of. I'm certainly not."

I was now lying my ass off.

The male in front of me didn't look the slightest bit convinced. No, instead, he stared down at me as if he could see right through me. I refused to look away. I might have been an Omega, but I wasn't in Moon-Ghost anymore. No one was going to push me around.

"Would it kill you to back up?" I asked. Seriously, one half-step and we'd be chest to chest. My neck was going to cramp soon.

From this distance, his scent teased my nose. I couldn't put my finger on the scent, but it didn't seem odd that I would lack the words to describe it. It was masculine, though. Like running through the deep woods. I resisted the urge to lean in and sniff.

"I don't see why I should move an inch, given that this is my room, in my home. You certainly took your time exploring."

His high and mighty tone made my skin bristle. "If you didn't want me wandering around, you should've said something sooner." Clearly, he'd known I was there even if I hadn't realized he was.

His lips curved just into the barest hint of a smirk. "And miss the show?"

I will not blush, I will not blush... It was a colossal effort to not look away. Specifically, to look down at the hastily buttoned shirt—his shirt—that I was wearing. But for all my internal chanting, my cheeks turned into little flames.

"Perv," I ground out.

"Thief," he countered.

And we were at an impasse. Neither of us willing to break gazes, neither of us apologizing.

The male in front of me didn't have a submissive bone in his body, that much was clear. Dominance seemed to roll off him in waves, threatening to take me under.

But I didn't want to submit. If anything, it made me want to stand my ground more.

We might've stood there forever, glaring, seething.

But then, to my mortification, my stomach growled.

And it wasn't a quiet growl. Not a little rumble that could be easily ignored. No, it was a five-excruciating-second low moan. Because while I was trying to stare down the most dominant male I'd ever come across, my stomach had to compose a sonnet about how empty it was.

The male blinked. I wanted to cheer at the victory, but it felt a bit hollow when I wanted to curl up into a ball of mortification.

"You're... hungry." He spoke the words slowly as if he couldn't understand them. Somehow, the words lacked the usual mocking tone.

Apparently, I wasn't full from a single rabbit in... what had it been, two days? "Not really."

"Very convincing," he said, mimicking my earlier taunt. "When did you last eat?"

When he asked, there was almost something familiar about his voice. The words. The concern.

But I was imagining it. I was reading in kindness where a stranger just had idle curiosity.

"I'm not sure." It was the first honest, nonconfrontational thing I'd said and the male in front of me almost seemed surprised I'd answered him. "It's hard for me to tell in this realm, or whatever you called it."

There was silence for a beat, the slight narrowing of his brows as he examined me. Then, without warning, he turned. He reached the doorframe and spoke, not looking back at me or breaking stride. "Come, little wolf. I'll give you something to eat."

It was my turn to blink. That was all I could do, staring at his back before shuffling after him across the cold floor. He was halfway down the hall when I caught up to him.

"Um, thanks," I said.

He didn't spare me a glance. "Think nothing of it. And I mean that literally."

Okay, so he was back to being an arrogant jerk. I wasn't even sure he'd stopped since he'd basically ordered me to follow him. I was too hungry to argue. Once my stomach sensed food on the horizon, it made its emptiness painfully clear.

I was no stranger to missed meals. The pack cafeteria was

my own personal torture chamber, so I avoided it as much as possible. Most of my former packmates were lean, but I was just scrawny. Daphne would steal bits of food for me when she could. She did her best to help me, even if it meant risking her own standing in the pack. Not for the first time, my chest ached at the thought of my friend.

We came to an abrupt stop in front of a door. It looked like any of the dozen locked ones I'd passed before, but the male opened the door with ease.

"Help yourself. It seems you're naturally inclined to, anyway," he added with a pointed look at my shirt.

I ignored him. Because he'd just opened the door to paradise.

It was a kitchen fit for a castle, but it was like a kitchen ready to lay out a feast. Every counter was filled with food. Roast meats and vegetables and piles of fruit. Shelves filled with every type of confection, from cakes to cookies to pies that made my mouth water. The longer I looked, the more I saw. Up high, there were bottles of wine. Between trays, there were smaller offerings, cheeses and grapes, and cured meats.

I breathed in the smells. Deliciousness. I could practically taste the cherry pie on my lips.

I took a step forward and hesitated.

"Is it safe?" I asked.

He shrugged. "As safe as anything in this realm can be."

That didn't tell me much.

There was something unnatural about the food. A room full of piping hot food enough to feed an army? And no one around to cook it?

But I was hungry. And some gut instinct told me it was okay. I took another step in and grabbed the nearest thing to me. A sandwich, which was the least exotic thing available and probably the most comfortable for me to eat.

The stranger didn't enter. He leaned against the door, arms folded across his bare chest, while he seemed to look everywhere but at me. It was like he was purposely keeping as much distance between us as possible.

Which was odd since, at first, he'd seemed almost playful. I could get whiplash trying to keep up. Let me tease you. No, intimidate you. No, offer you a sandwich that is bizarrely more delicious than any other sandwich in your memory.

"Aren't you going to join me?" I shifted on my feet, feeling awkward just standing in the room eating.

He didn't move an inch, but he finally met my gaze. "No."

I wrinkled my nose. I wasn't sure why it bothered me, but it did. "You're a crappy host."

"An unwilling one," he corrected.

Did he have to be such a jerk? It was like he was trying. Well, screw him.

Of course, at the thought, my mind decided to take liberties. Liberties that made me look his body up and down and imagine what it would be like. To have those arms around you, pinning you down. To taste that elusive scent... With a body and face like that, it was impossible not to imagine, just for a second.

"Are you thinking of devouring my pants for your third course?"

The cutting words jolted me out of my daydream, and I flushed. Seriously, what was wrong with me? I'd always scoffed at the phrase animal attraction. But damn. It hadn't even felt this way with the mate bond with Jett, however short-lived. He'd seemed perfect in the moment. Like a drug that lulled you into a warm embrace without you noticing you were suffocating.

Looking at this male? It was like pumping raw adrenaline into my veins.

"I was thinking you haven't introduced yourself," I said, trying to recover from my not-unnoticed eye-fuck.

"I haven't."

"No, you haven't. And since we've already established you're a terrible host, you might not realize it would be polite to. So let me explain. Normally, when two people meet, they exchange their names. It typically begins what is known as a conversation." And I desperately needed to talk to someone for answers before I went crazy.

"A lecture on manners from the woman who broke into my home."

"I didn't break—ugh." I rolled my eyes to the ceiling. "I'll go first. My name is Avery Ward." I gestured, inviting him to go.

"Cole." No last name. But it was something. Better than to keep calling him "the stranger" or "the male" in my head. Or "the most insufferable, dominant jerk I've ever met" if I was being honest.

"Nice to meet you, Cole."

He didn't echo the pleasantries, but I shrugged it off. "Well, Cole." I put extra emphasis on his name, earning a slightly raised brow. "Can you tell me where we are?"

"My castle."

"Yes, we've established that." I tried (and probably failed) not to sound impatient. "Can you go a bit farther than that?"

Was he deliberately obtuse?

"On my land," he said in that same monotone that made me want to tear my hair out.

"Yes, yes. We're in your castle, on your land, and where is that? You mentioned a realm before. What's this realm called?"

"The realm?" he repeated. "You don't know?"

"If I knew, I wouldn't be asking you the same question thirty different ways," I ground out. "I woke up on the ground in the middle of nowhere. Nothing is familiar. The scents are different, and I'm nowhere near my pack lands. You're the first creature I've come across who I could actually have a conversation with, even though that seems to be a stretch. So if you could be so kind as to enlighten me, I'd really freaking appreciate it."

Cole didn't speak for a moment. His eyes flashed bright, fixed on me, freezing me in place. He pushed himself off the wall and crossed the space between us in four smooth steps.

"Well, Avery Ward. Welcome to Hell."

CHAPTER XI

"HELL? YOU'RE JOKING, RIGHT?" Even as I said those words, a sinking feeling took over. Hadn't I had the same thought a dozen times since I'd woken up in that field?

"Consider yourself enlightened." There wasn't a trace of humor in his voice.

"That can't be. I mean... Why would I go to Hell?"

"Presumably because you died," Cole cut in.

"I'm not a bad person, though. And I don't even believe in Hell! Not for shifters, anyway. Not that I've thought about it a lot. That bitch of a moon goddess is supposed to put us up in the stars when we die."

He raised a brow at my description of the moon goddess but said nothing. I was on a roll now. And she was a bitch for pairing me and the alpha's son. Moon-matched my furry butt. "Besides, this can't be Hell. I mean, there's basically no one here. If I'm in Hell, then clearly the bar is pretty low for eternal damnation. Plus, Hell should be monstrous. Terrifying. Fire and brimstone, right? This place isn't horrible."

I was grasping at straws. Actually, I was panicking. Because this whole time, I'd had nothing to confirm or deny my worst fears.

But Cole had just told me my worst fear was true.

"Isn't it?" he said. He stood still, eyes catching every frantic movement while I paced back and forth in the kitchen.

"I mean, not really." My mind was happy to seize on a distraction. "Like I said, fire and brimstone, right? Okay, there's that weird lava moat you got going on, but I'm sure there's a logical explanation for that. You seem like the type who would do something dramatic like that in an intimidate-your-enemies mood"—another eyebrow quirk—"And sure, there was one blue demon-y type thing, but shifters look pretty gnarly when we change too. So I shouldn't judge. Everything else is normal. Normal-ish, I guess. That lake was pretty. I walked through fields of flowers. The trees look different, but it's not like they drink blood, right? The rabbit I ate didn't even give me indigestion."

His eyes narrowed. "Demon-y thing."

"I don't know. It was blue and had horns and didn't like me. You two have something in common."

Cole didn't deign to respond to the jab. "You'll have to get used to a lot worse than that if you're going to survive here."

Here. In Hell.

Slowly, the panicked energy faded and all I was left with was fear. Bone-deep fear as the reality sunk in. I stopped pacing around the kitchen and sunk into a wing-backed chair by a small table. To my surprise, Cole took the seat opposite me.

"Is that all you do here? Survive?" I asked.

"As opposed to what?"

"Live. Talk to people. Have a family." The things that filled the empty void in life. I'd spent most of my childhood surviving, but it had been bearable because I had Daphne. Daphne and the belief things wouldn't always be that way.

"I've no need for other people." He didn't look at me as he spoke. I frowned.

"Everyone needs someone to care about."

He looked at me directly then, and I almost flinched at the longing in his gaze. Then, a second later, it was gone. I was almost convinced I imagined it.

"Is there a way out of here?" I asked.

"The front door."

I rolled my eyes. "Not the castle. Out of Hell." Where I would go, I couldn't guess. But there was nothing for me here.

He looked about to say something, then changed his mind. "That's something you and every creature wants, but I doubt you'll find it. This is Hell, after all."

"That's not a no."

"It may as well be," he said, cutting down the bit of hope that had begun to grow. "There's no escaping this realm."

I sighed and pulled my legs up, hugging them against me. "Can you tell me more about what 'this realm' is? Is it as big as the continent? Are there cities? Are there other shifters?"

If I could find another pack, maybe I could get my fresh start anyway. Yes, Hell was supposed to be bad and evil and all that, but it didn't seem that bad. Maybe unconventional, but perhaps there was a way I could find a pack of my own here.

"The realm is infinite. I wouldn't recommend the cities. And no, you won't find other shifters. They tend to take... a different route."

"What does that mean?" I demanded.

He shrugged, looking like he didn't give a damn what demands I had. "Let's say some stories have a grain of truth."

A cryptic reply if ever there was one.

Suddenly, I was so tired. It was exhausting, always having more questions than answers. Lacking any certainty. It felt like I was walking through mud, constantly stumbling, getting nowhere, and slowly sinking deeper and deeper. My whole body ached, a product of too little sleep and everything else it had been through.

Cole sighed too. The slightest hint of exhaustion, though since he'd been laying in a comfortable bed rather than a cave floor, I couldn't imagine what his issue was. He stood from the chair in a single movement and looked down at me. He seemed to be deciding something, and I let him have his internal argument because I was too tired to tease out if it was for or against me.

"You can rest here for the night." Just like before, he started towards the door without so much as a backwards glance. I didn't bother to object because, honestly, a room sounded great.

It was weird, though. I should've seen him as a threat. He wasn't kind, not really. He led me through the winding corridors, opposite the way we'd come, and I examined him. He was bigger than me. Even with my newfound shifter strength, cold logic told me he could kill me without much effort. His moods turned quickly. I shouldn't let my guard down around him. Shouldn't have accepted food, shouldn't let him lead me through a labyrinth of stone halls which I had no way to escape.

But something deep down, more basic than even instinct, told me it was okay. Not that I was perfectly safe, but he wouldn't harm me.

"Here." Cole opened the door to a massive bedroom. Well, maybe not massive compared to the castle, but considering I'd been sleeping in a glorified shoe box my whole life, it was huge.

Twin to the one I'd found him in, the color scheme was black, red, and gold. Dark oak furniture lined the room without coming close to filling it. Large, stain-glass windows lined the other side. There was an en suite bathroom, which definitely seemed like a luxury after the past few days in the woods. But most of all, the bed looked amazing. King-sized and made with a half dozen pillows, I couldn't wait to sink under the covers.

"Thank you," I said, remembering my manners. "This looks great." Even if it was in Hell.

"Don't thank me. This is for one night only. Tomorrow morning, you leave."

This time, I wasn't able to stop from flinching at the harshness of his words. It wasn't that he owed me a place to stay. I had, after all, just barged into his home. But with the food, the room... he'd seemed nice. Well, at least a bit nice under the prickliness of a cactus.

"Fine." I didn't thank him again, just went into the room and flopped on the bed. It was like sinking into a cloud. I nearly passed out on the spot. When was the last time I'd been this comfortable? Maybe never. "Are you going to stand there all night?" I asked, peeling my head slightly off the mattress.

Cole was still in the doorway. Watching. Contemplating killing me?

A crazy part of me thought of inviting him to bed. After all, I was dead. What was the worst that could happen?

But two things stopped me.

One, I was ninety-nine percent sure he wouldn't kill me in my sleep. That last percent was going to have me barricading the door the second I went to bed. Years of abuse led to enough wariness that instinct meant nothing.

And two, I doubted the attraction went both ways. Even

if he alternated between abrasive and downright mean, Cole was physical perfection. And it was more than his body—the way he moved said he knew it. He was the king of the castle, and goddess help anyone in his way.

Me? I wasn't ugly, but I was scrawny. I moved without the natural grace of most shifters. And I was newly dead.

Still, Cole watched me. Another of those invisible wars was waged behind amber eyes, and I was too tired to decipher it.

"If you're only giving me one night, I'd like to sleep as much as possible. So, shoo." I lifted my hand and waved him away for emphasis.

His lips twitched, but whether it was a frown or smile, I didn't see before he turned.

Once he was gone, I shut the door and lodged a chair under the handle. Too tired to examine the rest of the room, I crawled under the covers.

And I let sleep take me away.

I T WAS A RARE, dreamless night.

It made for an unsettling sleep. I was used to that voice in my dreams and looked forward to it, even if it was nothing more than a simple dream. Sometimes teasing, sometimes chiding, the voice was always a comfort. It found me whether I was stuffed in a middle school locker overnight or sleeping in my own home.

Despite that, I was well-rested. I woke up at what must've been dawn, based on the lightening sky.

Hell. I was in Hell.

Last night, I'd had a range of reactions. Denial. Panic.

Today, there was just acceptance. Yes, I was in Hell.

Well, so what? I'd dealt with worse. I'd been bullied for more than half my life, forsaken by my moon-matched mate, murdered by my own packmates, and while I hadn't exactly survived, I was still myself. I wasn't broken.

And I wasn't going to let this realm break me.

I forced myself out of the bed, shivering as my feet landed on the cold floor. I made a mental note to tell Cole to use some of the lava moat for castle heating.

Really, though, I was stalling. The castle had been a brief reprieve. Nothing more.

I was still in Cole's shirt from yesterday. I resisted the temptation to smell it, checking for more of that heady, masculine scent that was so intoxicating. Okay, mostly resisted. One little sniff.

I hated that I liked his scent so much.

It was at once familiar, yet mysterious. Sensual. Powerful. It was his essence, and even if I didn't understand all the layers, I knew it was him.

But he meant nothing to me. Or at least, he shouldn't. I'd barely met him. Didn't even know what kind of creature he was. What he'd done to land himself in Hell.

In the daylight, I examined the room more closely. I freshened up in the en suite bathroom and almost sighed in relief when I found there was hot running water. I didn't care how it was possible, just that I wanted to dance in delight under the hot spray. Washing the grime out of my hair was practically a religious experience. I roughly towel-dried it, then went looking for an alternative to the shirt. There was a dresser tucked against one wall.

And it had women's clothing. Not just women's clothing, clothes in my size. I found a black tank top and matching pants that fit me too perfectly to be a coincidence. The sneakers were even the right size. I frowned at the barricaded door.

It didn't look like it had been disturbed. Besides, there was no way someone could've gotten in without knocking it over and waking me up.

I forced myself to shrug it off and accept it. Based on yesterday's feat, this realm didn't play by the continent's rules. The trick would be to learn them since my only potential source of information seemed to hate having me under the same roof.

Turning my attention back to the dresser, I found a red leather jacket. I shrugged it on, immediately feeling warmer.

Well, no sense wasting daylight, even if I wanted to linger. I left the bedroom in search of Cole.

It didn't take long to track him down. I was wandering through the hallways, trying to retrace our steps and decide if the weird stone statues were actually familiar or if they just looked similar to the other hundred of them when I rounded a corner—

And slammed right into Cole.

"Yowch!" I stumbled back and lost my balance. Air whooshed around me as I fell. I braced for impact with the hard, stone floor.

But it never came.

Instead, two hands caught my arms and pulled me up.

As suddenly as I'd been falling, I was chest-to-chest with Cole.

Whoops.

I looked up at him, ignoring the embarrassed flush of my cheeks. "Good morning," I said weakly. From the distance, I couldn't help but breathe in his scent. The shirt had the barest echo of it. This was like a straight hit. One inhale and the last remnants of sleepiness were gone, replaced by anticipation.

There's nothing to anticipate! I reminded myself.

"We'll see."

I exhaled through my nose, grasping for patience. "What's up your butt? If you're this grumpy after a full night's sleep, I can understand why you were so mad about me interrupting your nap yesterday."

Damn that infuriating eyebrow that crept up. "I didn't realize you were such a morning person."

"Didn't realize?" I repeated, looking up at him in disbelief.

"Not sure how you'd know anything about me since you haven't asked me a single question."

"You're right." He stepped back abruptly, nearly sending me off balance again. "Because I don't care, little wolf. You're on your own here, not in the coddled safety of your pack, and you'd best remember that."

Coddled safety? This guy didn't know anything about what I'd been through.

But I didn't correct him because, like he'd just said, he didn't give a shit.

And damn if that didn't somehow sting.

"Fine. Show me the door then."

"And here I thought you'd want to gorge yourself again."

He was right. I was hungry. I shouldn't refuse to eat for spite, not when I didn't know how long it'd be until the next meal.

But useless pride kept me from backtracking. "The door, Cole. Then you can get back to whatever delightful things you get up to all by yourself in this stupid castle, and for the record, my name is 'Avery' not 'little wolf.'"

Cole didn't answer, but he listened. A few minutes down winding hallways and we were at the massive wooden doors I'd pushed open just last night.

My pulse beat faster. It had been one thing to explore outside when I'd been forced to. What other choice had I had? But now, I'd known safety, even if just for a short while, and it was hard for me to force myself to face that unknown danger again.

Cole had no such reservations about kicking me out. He pulled a door open without an ounce of hesitation, then looked at me expectantly.

I met those amber eyes, and I felt more vulnerable than ever before. "What am I supposed to do now?" I wasn't sure why I asked. What answer could he give me?

Despite the morning's animosity, his answer was soft. "The same thing the rest of us do, Avery. Survive."

Chapter XII

D ay Three in Hell was off to a terrific start.

Survive. Fine for him to say with his castle full of magic food and comfortable beds.

I still had so many questions, and I regretted not asking more last night. No shifters, he'd said, but there were people, and people congregated. Surely not every single person lived alone.

And then... then I'd figure it out.

In retrospect, I might have been just as lost if I had been paired with a moon-matched mate in another pack. Up until then, my days were filled with attending classes and dodging bullies. I'd been surviving then too, but I'd survived with a purpose—to join a new pack. After that, I didn't know. I wasn't skilled at any particular trade. I'd have a family, eventually, but I'd need more than that. No disrespect to the shifters who stayed home with their children, but children eventually grew up. I'd definitely need more than that.

I felt like I was back at square one. Shelter, food, and water were the top priorities, but I needed to get farther away, to find others. I didn't want to live the rest of my life as a lone wolf.

I didn't want to be alone.

Well, they say the journey of a thousand miles begins with a single step, and by 'they' I meant some inspirational poster I'd read at school.

Without the sun, I had no way to tell direction. I looked back at the castle one last time. It was even bigger than I'd realized the night before. Where would Cole be now, I wondered. I might not find it again. Find him.

But it didn't matter. He didn't matter.

I headed to the right of the castle and started walking. Changing into my wolf form would be faster, but then I'd lose the clothing I'd finally gotten, so it was going to be a slow journey on two legs.

The first few hours passed surprisingly quickly, with me mostly being lost in my own thoughts. Rabbits were scattered through the grassy areas, more plentiful than I'd initially realized. That was promising. Nothing larger crossed my path, though.

If this was Hell, there was no way it was empty. What kind of person I'd meet, though, I couldn't guess.

I paused for a break after cresting the most recent hill and wiped a thin layer of sweat from my brow. This part of the land was hilly, so more of my time was spent going up and down than any real distance.

From my vantage point, I scanned the surrounding area. Woods farther ahead on the right, a thin stream flowing near the edge.

I swallowed involuntarily. I was parched. If I got to the river, I could drink my fill, catch some dinner later along it, and settle myself in a tree to sleep when night fell. Just having a plan made me feel better.

My attention snagged on something farther down the river. I squinted. There, on the side of the river bank... there was smoke! I strained as much as I could. A campfire. That meant people.

Excitement lit through me. This was the first sign of normalcy I'd had since coming here. No strange empty castle, no murderous blue monster. Someone had set up a small base. If I could just reach them, maybe they could help me. Feeling renewed hope, I started down the hill.

The river was wider than it had looked at a distance. It was easily twenty feet across at its narrowest, the bends winding their way around. I followed it, confident I would see other people soon.

It took almost the full day to the camp. I hoped it wasn't abandoned. No one was nearby, but smoke still clung to the air. It was a recent fire.

I eased closer to look around.

Definitely recent. The ground was more wet on the side of the river, and I saw footprints. I followed the tracks. They led over to the river. I frowned, looking over. Could they have crossed to the forest side? I wasn't sure how they'd have managed. The river was fast-moving and I couldn't see the bottom.

"Help! I'm drowning! Save me!"

Shit. I jumped back at the desperate plea. There, about thirty feet from me. Someone was caught in the river. I couldn't make out a clear shape, but they flailed in desperation. The current carried them farther and farther out and threatened to drown them entirely.

I had to help.

I sprinted along the bank.

"Help me!" Another terrified plea.

"Hang on!" I called.

They were about six, seven feet from the shore. I looked around for something I could pass them. A branch or something they could grab onto. But the field was empty.

Shit. They were moving farther under, only the hands breaking the surface now.

There was no time. They needed help.

I only had one choice.

I dove in.

"Grab my hand!" I yelled, trying to be heard over the river's rapids. God, how had it seemed so quiet just moments ago?

I kicked out farther, trying to reach them.

I was within arms reach. I grabbed for them, fighting

against the current to stay above water.

They clasped my hand.

I breathed a sigh of relief. I'd reached them. It would be okay.

Then they dragged me under.

CHAPTER XIII

I GASPED IN SURPRISE. A critical mistake.

Water immediately rushed into my opened mouth. I was choking on the water, drowning myself, and could do nothing to stop it. My lungs burned, my whole body fighting against the intrusion.

And I was being dragged deeper.

I forced my eyes open. There, the would-be drowning victim. A girl, no older than ten. She wasn't human. And she was damn strong. Webbed fingers grasped my wrist, pulling and pulling.

No. No, no, no.

I panicked, the flailing getting worse while I couldn't breathe. Wildly, I kicked at her arm. Her grip broke, and I breached the surface long enough to sputter and get one breath of air before I was being pulled again, this time by the leg.

Survive. I had to survive.

I kicked like hell, but her webbed grip wouldn't budge. I changed tactics. I couldn't let her keep me underwater. I wasn't a swimmer. I sure as shit didn't have gills. I needed air, so I forced both of us up to the surface.

Then down again.

A constant struggle, over and over. Adrenaline pushed me through the wave of exhaustion that slammed into me.

Then, the grip released.

I kicked to the surface and swam for the bank. Five feet. Four. Almost there. Three. Just a few more seconds...

The webbed hands were back. And they were around my neck.

I cried out in surprise, trying to kick off the she-creature, but her grip was firm. There was no escape.

No. She couldn't win. But my movements were slow. Her grip tightened, and it was impossible to breathe. She was choking me.

Then, a flash of black. The grip released. It didn't matter. I couldn't even tread water. My body was foreign, my brain lost in the suffocated fog.

But then I was yanked up. Something gripped me by the jacket, pulling, forcing me towards the bank. Not the she-beast. No, whatever had chased it off.

It didn't stop until I was dragged onto the bank. I knelt, bent over my knees, coughing water out of my lungs. I shook my head, trying to clear the blurriness that had come from oxygen deprivation. I thought I would vomit, but the bile held in the back of my throat, unwilling to dislodge.

And then I raised my head and looked at my savior.

A wolf.

Not just any wolf. It towered over me, kneeling, but it would've been my height standing easily. It was the biggest wolf I'd ever seen. Even bigger than Maddox in his wolf form. Midnight-black fur, sleek from the trip in the river. But even with that, it was a majestic creature. Yellow eyes that seemed to glow in the evening light were trained on me.

"Y–you saved m–me." I shivered. The river had been freezing, and I was soaked. Exhausted. Was everything in this realm going to have a go at killing me? Was it going to eat me now?

I wanted to lie down and sleep. The dirt suddenly seemed inviting.

The wolf abruptly shook itself, a massive movement that sent water flying everywhere, including right on me.

I couldn't even muster the energy to protest.

The wolf took a step towards me. Slow, almost cautious. When I didn't move, it got closer until we were nose-to-nose.

"Th–thanks," I said. "I'm g–good now."

The wolf crouched down in front of me, moving so its body was in front of me.

I frowned, not knowing what it wanted.

When I didn't move, the wolf turned back and nudged my hands. It seemed to shake its head to the back, gesturing for me to do something.

"Y–you want me to get on your back?" I asked.

The wolf crouched lower in invitation. Apparently, I'd finally gotten the message.

It wasn't like I had any better ideas. I eased off my knees and moved to straddle the wolf. Even with it lying down, it was a struggle. Once I was settled, the wolf stood effortlessly. I wrapped my arms around its neck, and then the wolf took off.

It was bizarre to ride a wolf since normally I just turned into one.

Then again, it was less a ride and more me holding on for dear life.

Shifters were fast, even faster than normal wolves. But this creature moved like the wind. The hills that had taken me hours to climb were crossed in just minutes. It was a miracle I didn't fall off.

Just another weird day in Hell. I was becoming numb to the craziness of the realm. What would tomorrow bring to top this?

Or at least, I thought I was getting numb to it until I saw where the wolf was taking me.

No way. I groaned as Cole's castle came into view. "Take me somewhere else," I demanded.

Or tried. It's kind of hard to demand anything when you're holding onto a two-hundred-and-fifty-pound wolf for dear life.

My request was ignored, the wolf running all the way to

the moat and then marching me across the drawbridge. We reached the massive wooden doors, and the wolf lowered itself so I could stand.

Immediately, I tried walking back across the drawbridge. The wolf blocked my path.

Great. Just great.

Still shivering, I made my way to the door. I expected it to be locked—really, Cole should've learned by now—but it wasn't. I shoved the wooden door open, though it was more of a tap in my current condition.

But the door spread wide nonetheless.

I entered, and the wolf followed. I looked around for any sign of Cole. Relieved he wasn't in the immediate vicinity, I turned around to tell the wolf that this was obviously a bad idea and I'd figure something else out.

And was suddenly face-to-face with Cole.

A very, very naked Cole.

I did what any other composed shifter with lightning-fast reflexes would do.

I let out an ear-splitting shriek.

The wolf. Cole was the wolf who had saved me.

"What the f–fuck? You're a shifter?" He'd said there weren't any down here. Liar.

"'What the fuck' indeed," he growled, and it was an animalistic sound. One designed to strike fear into the hearts of enemies. It had a slightly different effect on me. "What were you thinking, diving into the river after a nixie?"

I didn't even know what that was. "I thought someone was drowning. How was I supposed to know?"

"You're supposed to know because you're in Hell, Avery! If someone tells you they're drowning, you let them because they're going to stab you in the back at the first chance they get."

Oh, didn't he think he knew everything? "That might b–be who you are, but that's not who I am. Besides, why do you care? You kicked me out this morning." My voice continued to shake from the cold, made worse by his miserably unheated castle. My clothes felt like an icy straight jacket. At least, I told myself it was the cold. Not that I was in any way hurt, he'd sent me on my way without so much as a "hope you don't drown."

"I don't care," Cole insisted. His voice was barely leashed fury. "I just didn't feel like picking your bones off my front lawn when the nixie was done using them as toothpicks."

"Front lawn? I was miles away. H––how'd you even know I w–was there?"

"That doesn't matter." I opened my mouth to argue, but he cut me off. "What matters is getting you out of those clothes. You're halfway to hypothermia, and if you stay like this much longer your lungs could take a hit."

Why do you care? It was on the tip of my tongue to ask again, but like he'd said, he didn't care. He just rescued me from being drowned by evil mermaids in the river to keep fit or something.

And... He was *fit*. I'd had a peek yesterday with him shirtless, but Cole, naked... Every inch of muscled flesh exposed. The tattoo I'd spied before crept down farther and my gaze followed it. Lower and lower...

And then slingshot back up. *Focus on his face, Avery!*

But from the expression on his face, I wasn't the only one staring. The water made my tank top cling to my skin, molding around my curves. The cold had certainly had an effect on me beyond nearly making me freeze to death. At least, I hoped that was why my nipples were rock-hard.

I crossed my arms defensively over my chest. "Are you volunteering another of your shirts? They seem to be in short supply around here."

"It's hard when people steal them."

Now it was my turn to growl. Growl and ignore the way his gaze made me feel. The way it made me want to arch my back despite the cold.

"Well, I'll need something warm because this castle is so cold I'm liable to get frostbite standing here bickering with you."

Cole frowned at me, then sighed. "Just come with me."

He walked past me, beginning one of his typical lead-Avery-somewhere-without-a-glance-back tours he was so fond of.

There was one perk to his not-looking-back, though.

I had an unbeatable view. I didn't consider myself much of an ass-woman but, well, Cole made me re-examine that stance. Because talk about a butt. Firm, sculpted. It was like something off a statue.

Well, not one of these statues. We passed a corner with a three-headed monkey. A nice Greek statue. The kind that made you understand why they were almost all into men.

And just like that, we were in a bedroom that looked all too familiar.

Did he think... An irrational, stupid jolt went through me at the thought of sharing a bed with Cole. At the thought of breaking that same bed with him.

But then he went over to his wardrobe and pulled out a knit mass of yarn. He tossed it to me and I caught it, unfolding the lump that definitely hadn't been in there yesterday.

"Is there an ugly sweater contest I need to win to leave this place or something? If so, thanks for the winning ticket."

"You said you were cold. It's warm." So stop complaining was the subtext.

Fine. I turned my back to the infuriating male and shucked off my wet shirt and jacket. The tank top practically had to be pried off, and I was pretty sure I ripped the wet fabric in the process. I couldn't even muster the energy to feel bad. I was just too cold for that.

Once that was done, I slipped the sweater on. The sweater,

despite being a cross between puke green and moldy blue, was actually super soft and warm. It just had the side effect of hiding my body under one giant lump of wool.

I turned back... and found Cole's gaze fixed on me.

"Take a picture. It lasts longer," I said, cheeks heating at the thought of him watching me undress, even if only for a second. Shifters weren't by nature squeamish about naked bodies—it was only natural, after all—but my body was keenly aware of Cole's gaze. I'd assumed he wasn't interested and hadn't hesitated to get out of the wet clothes, but nothing in his gaze right then made me think uninterested.

For his part, he'd also slipped on a sweater, though it was a thinner-knit and fit his body like a glove, showing off the definition in his biceps. He'd also put on a pair of pants.

"Do I get some of those?" I asked. "Pants?" I clarified to his raised brow.

The only answering sound was the thwack as a thick, woolen pair hit me square in the chest. I debated changing into them right away because soggy pants are as fun as my old pack alpha. But then Cole would see me, and I didn't have any underwear on. On the other hand, there was the en suite, but I'd feel like an idiot walking past him to change.

I debated for a solid three seconds. Then my need for privacy won out, and I darted past him, shutting the door firmly behind me.

I changed quickly and looked myself over in the mirror. I

was no fashionista, but had he actually tried to dress me in the ugliest combination of clothing known to man? The clothes were warm, but several sizes too big. Maybe even bigger than Cole. They swallowed me. And that was to say nothing of the way they clashed. Weird because Cole looked perfectly fine.

More than fine, actually.

I tried not to picture him when he'd revealed himself—well, in both senses of the word. People weren't supposed to look like that. That perfect. Everyone had at least one decent flaw. Crooked teeth, relentless sideburns. A scratchy voice or weirdly shaped fingers. A small dick. Something to keep us humble.

There was nothing humble about Cole. Or Cole's dick as I'd learned and couldn't stop thinking about and *oh my goddess why was I still in this bathroom thinking about the man's cock?*

"Is there a problem?" an annoyed voice growled through the door.

And said perfect-down-to-his-dick man was outside.

Actually, I took it back. He did have a flaw. It was his grumpy, inhospitable personality. Yes, he'd saved me for some inexplicable reason. But he'd also kicked me out.

"Don't worry, you'll have your bathroom back in a second." I pushed off the countertop and swung open the door, coming face-to-face with a distinctly displeased-looking Cole. "You'll have your whole castle back when I leave."

"Leave?"

"I'm sure you can't wait to show me the door again, but I think I'll be able to find it myself." I tried to brush past him and leave the bedroom, but he moved to block me. Suddenly we were chest to chest again, those amber eyes fixed on me in a way that made me freeze in place.

"You're staying, little wolf."

Chapter XIV

"**I** told you not to call me that," I growled without much heat. I was too busy wondering how Cole had gone from shoving me out the door to informing me I was staying. "And if I want to leave, I damn well will."

He arched a brow at me. "You'd prefer to let some other creature kill you and toss your useless remains in my yard?"

I gnashed my teeth in frustration. "Maybe you could've mentioned there were weird murder mermaids in the rivers."

"It's Hell, Avery. Everyone and everything will try to kill you."

So he remembered my name. "Including you?"

Cole didn't answer. He just looked me over and somehow, despite the big, bulky sweater, I felt more exposed than ever.

"It's not safe," he repeated.

Now it was my turn to arch a brow. "Oh, was it safe this morning when you all but shoved me out the door?"

He shrugged in that infuriating, arrogant way that made me want to kick his shins. "I overestimated your ability to survive."

"Are you fucking kidding me right now?" There was no mistaking it. I was baring my teeth now.

My wolf stirred under my skin as if sensing a fight. My blood hummed, simmering. I'd never thought of myself as much of a fighter, but Cole brought out the side even when he—objectively—was helping me.

"Control yourself." He sounded bored.

I took a step forward, my skin bristling, starting to ripple with the threat of turning. Who did he think he was, bossing me around?

My wolf wanted out. She wanted to lunge at him, sink her teeth into his flesh, and I was inclined to let her.

I'd been attacked today. I was in an unknown land, where, according to Cole, everything could and would try to kill me. I was cornered, and my wolf didn't like feeling cornered.

My fangs began to elongate, deepening my growl. The first sign of the change.

"Control yourself," he repeated, throwing so much dominance into the command my shift actually halted.

The command broke through the haze of aggression, and I actually stumbled. I put a hand on my forehead, trying to steady myself.

"What was that?" I asked, more to myself than Cole directly. The wolf had taken over, and I'd been powerless to stop her.

"I take it you didn't shift much growing up."

Hardly at all. "What does that have to do with anything?"

Cole pinched the bridge of his nose as if he had to count to ten before answering my question because it was so stupid.

"You're completely out of sync with your wolf. One of you is in charge at all times, and who that gets to be can switch very quickly, especially when you're under a lot of stress. Your wolf is more ruled by instincts, which can be especially overpowering—the urge to fight, to fuck, to hunt. Without training, they can overpower your rational side in a heartbeat. It will get better, but it takes time. It's important to minimize shocks to the system, like almost dying and freezing to death."

Oh. Come to think of it, I had heard about that growing up, but since my wolf form was so weak, I hadn't been able to put any of the lessons into practice and subsequently had quickly forgotten them.

"Hunger too. I suppose if I don't want you wrecking my house, I should feed you again."

He talked about me like an unwieldy pet. Maybe that was actually an accurate comparison in his mind. I would've complained, but now that he mentioned it, I was starving. Still lulled from the dominance of his command, I didn't feel angry.

He was already headed out the door, probably to the kitchen, so I raced after him to catch up.

"You're a wolf shifter. Like me." I'd been too distracted by our bickering to realize the full implications of that until now.

Not only that, but Cole was an alpha. There was no doubt in my mind about that. Maddox, and to a lesser extent, Jett, could imbue their commands with raw dominance. Less dominant wolves were compelled to obey, but in those cases, it was still possible to fight it off. I never fought back, but I'd been aware of their will trying to overpower mine, and deep down, I'd thought we could all push back—it was just a matter of not doing so out of respect.

But that wasn't what Cole's had felt like. No, if Maddox was a hammer pushing my will down, Cole was a freaking anvil.

"Something like that."

"Why didn't you tell me?" I pressed. "Why don't you have a pack?"

Being a lone wolf was a painful thing for shifters. It could drive them mad if left alone too long. But Cole was grouchy, not insane. At least, I didn't think so.

"I told you, there're no shifters here."

"But there are other creatures," I pointed out. "It's not the same, but everyone needs a pack."

I'd truly grown to hate Moon-Ghost, but at least within it, I'd had Daphne. If I hadn't had her, I wasn't sure I would've made it through adolescence.

Well, her and that weird subconscious voice. That had felt like a packmate too, which actually might have been a sign I was insane—inventing packmates where I'd had none.

He pushed open the kitchen door without a backward glance.

"Plus, I'm here. So I don't know how you can keep saying there're no shifters when there are at least two of us," I continued, only half paying attention now that I was back inside the kitchen, my personal happy place.

I started eating the first thing I could get my hands on, which turned out to be a plate full of brownies. Yum.

"There's no 'us.'" Cole's words were arctic.

There was no dignified way to growl at him with a mouth full of gooey chocolate, so I settled for rolling my eyes.

Then I shoved a brownie at him.

He looked at it with so much distrust I had to laugh.

"What?" he demanded.

"I think you're hungry too. You probably burned a million calories between diving into the freezing water after me and dragging me back here. Maybe your wolf is grumpy too."

"I'm not grumpy," he said in a grumpy voice. But he took the brownie.

We ate in silence for a couple minutes, and now that we weren't trading barbs, it was almost peaceful.

What a week. Finding my moon-matched mate, being rejected, being murdered, finally shifting properly, navigating Hell, stumbling onto this place, nearly drowning...

I frowned. "Wait. Can I die?" It said a lot that I still hadn't processed the implications of dying. "I mean, haven't I already done that once?"

Cole didn't speak for a long moment. "It's complicated."

It's complicated, or as I liked to translate it, I know the answers and I don't feel like sharing.

"It's kind of critical information for me to know, and you, you know, with the whole picking-my-bones-off-your-yard shtick."

Cole sighed. For the first time, he seemed almost to sag. My eyes latched onto the movement. In the brief time since I'd met Cole, he didn't sag or slouch. His posture was always immaculate, towering over me like a general ready to go to war.

"The short answer is yes, you can be killed."

"And then what happens?"

"The soul goes somewhere worse."

"Worse?" Getting answers was like pulling teeth.

"Tartarus." I frowned. I wasn't up to date on mythology, but that didn't seem to jive with us already being in Hell. As if sensing my next question, Cole sighed. "Death is a complicated thing. There are no other shifters here—and where their souls go, I couldn't tell you. This is Hell, but there's a level beneath us, so to speak. That is Tartarus. There are many more realms of the dead, a complicated web-based on magical species and so on, but these two are the ones that matter. Hell may be unpleasant, but Tartarus is unending torture. Take my word for it, you want to avoid being killed and sent there."

Which still begged the question why I was here. He claimed that we were the only two shifters—why us? Why me?

But I could understand the severity of what Cole told me; as bad as things were here, they could be worse, and while I didn't relish an eternity of surviving, it sure as shit would beat an eternity of torture.

That didn't mean I was going to give up on getting out of Hell. But clearly I still had a lot to learn about this realm.

CHAPTER XV

COLE DEPOSITED ME BACK in the same room I'd spent the night before in. I'd passed out almost as soon as my head hit the pillow, falling into another dreamless sleep. As ever, I found the absence disconcerting. One more missing comfort.

But when dawn broke and light flickered in, I awoke with a single purpose in mind.

I needed to get stronger.

Cole had been right—I was completely out of sync with my wolf. I was weak. Whatever had changed by coming to Hell made my wolf close to the surface at all times when, before she'd been buried, I needed to acclimate and to acclimate fast.

Which is why, starting today, I resolved to start training.

I had a lot of years to catch up on.

I changed out of the ugly, bulky sweater Cole had all but shoved me in yesterday and pulled out a comfortable set of clothes from the dresser, a pair of sweats and another tank top.

I left the room, first finding my way to the kitchen after a few dozen wrong turns, each one punctuated by one of those bizarre statues. Once my stomach was satisfied by half a dozen hard-boiled eggs and toast, I was ready to begin.

What I needed was a place to train. Of course I had no hopes of finding a gym, but that was probably way too much to ask for from an ancient castle. I checked room after room, but none were particularly suited to my purposes.

"Looking for something?" a low rumble asked.

"How did you sneak up on me?" I demanded, spinning around.

And it was good I spoke before actually looking because, damn. Cole was mere feet behind me, shirtless, with low-slung pants and mussed-up hair as if he'd just rolled out of bed. Out of bed after a satisfying night.

He was a good-looking male, no doubt. But more than that, there was a seductive edge etched into every aspect of his features. You looked at him and you thought about him in bed. And on the floor. And against the walls.

"Unlike you, I don't make a habit of stomping around like a wobbly elephant."

Annnnnnd there it was. I went thinking of him taking me against a wall to wanting to shove his skull into one.

"I'm looking for a place to train." I chose to let the barb go since, at the moment, I was hoping he'd help me find a viable spot.

"Train," he repeated.

"I thought about what you said yesterday," I explained. "About not being in sync with my wolf. I was... weak before I came here. Barely shifted into my wolf form, and I couldn't access much in the way of shifter strength."

How it hurt to admit that. Especially to Cole, who had probably never felt weak or powerless a day in his life. But I needed his help.

For a split second, something like approval flashed across his features. Then he turned, gesturing for me to follow in that infuriating way of his.

He led me up a long, winding flight of stairs. The castle had three levels, based on the exits of the staircase. But we went beyond that, all the way to the top.

The morning air was crisp, sending a brief chill down my spine while I took in where he'd led me to.

The rooftop was massive. I'd known the castle was large, but standing atop it put it in an entirely different perspective. I could run proper laps across the perimeter.

But more than that... It was an actual gym. Or a type of one. Not the entire area, but a solid quarter of the space was devoted to gym equipment. There was a bench with a bar and weights. An old-fashioned punching bag.

"Do you use this?" I asked.

"No, actually. I set this all up for decoration," Cole said, sarcasm dripping off his tongue.

"I don't understand. How'd you get all this?" I'd been

thrust into this realm without even the charity of the clothes on my back when I died. How was it possible?

"Just like with your clothing and the food you've been devouring, the castle provides. It senses its—" He hesitated, considering the next word carefully "—residents's needs. And so it provides."

I nodded like this all made perfect sense. "Gotcha. It said you were hitting the brownies too hard and set this up for you one day. Subtle, but thoughtful."

Now Cole rolled his eyes openly. "Enjoy."

I expected him to leave, but he didn't. Instead, he settled on the edge of the castle wall, surveying the area.

Whatever. This was exactly what I'd wanted and never expected to find—a proper gym.

That said, for all my determination, I didn't know much about how to work out. The Moon-Ghost pack gym had been a hotbed of dominance fights and all-around aggression, so I'd steered clear of that. I'd skipped most phys ed classes, and the teachers hadn't even bothered to chastise me since they knew I wouldn't be able to keep up with the rest of the adolescent shifters. Daphne and I had been more inclined to bake muffins than go for runs together. Besides, all shifters preferred to run in their wolf forms, and that hadn't been an option for me.

I stretched on the padded surface while thinking of my game plan. I was curious about how strong I was as a shifter.

Barbell it was then.

The barbell was already loaded with a couple plates. Might as well start there—nothing would make me happier than to be able to lift as much as the smug, dominant wolf who was currently very much not looking at me. Not that I was super aware of his gaze or anything.

I bent down and tried to lift.

The bar didn't so much as budge.

I tried harder, straining my arms as I gripped the bar with all my strength. Still nothing. Seriously, just one inch and I'd call it a victory at this point.

"What could you possibly be trying to accomplish?"

Apparently, Cole had given up on his whole staring-off-into-the-distance thing and wanted to criticize me.

"I'm checking how strong I am." The skepticism on his face didn't do wonders for my confidence. I huffed. "It's harder than it looks."

Cole stepped closer until we were inches apart. From this distance, I could breathe in his scent in full force.

He wrestled the bar from my hands where my wrists were currently screaming.

Then he lifted the bar in one smooth motion. The bastard didn't even break a sweat.

Well, shit. There went any hope of us being equally strong as shifters.

He dropped the bar lightly on the rooftop, but even that

gentle fall let out a loud thud on the stone.

I finally read the numbers on the plates—and holy shit. That bar had three hundred pounds on each side.

"Show-off," I groused.

Cole didn't deign to reply. Instead, he set about taking off the plates. Two-thirds of them to be precise.

"Try now," he instructed.

I wanted to ignore the command just to be contrary, but even I could tell that was childish. I bent down again to lift and he stopped me.

"Not like that. Lift with your knees." He demonstrated.

I adjusted my stance and tried again. This time, I was able to comfortably lift the weight.

Well, not exactly comfortably, but my pride refused to let my arms wobble under Cole's demanding gaze.

"Thanks." At least I had a benchmark now.

I expected Cole to go back to his post at the wall, but he didn't move.

"This won't help you and your wolf harmonize."

Who asked you? I bit back the retort. I was frustrated with myself, really. And Cole knew a lot more about this than I did.

"I figured strengthening my human form would translate into strengthening my wolf," I said, still a bit defensive.

Cole nodded. "In the long run, you're right. But your is-sue—at least, your main one—isn't strength. It's the fact you have no control. No sense of when you should rely on the wolf, no way to work in sync."

I sighed. He was probably right. After all this time, the truth was, I was still a bit scared of my wolf. Yes, it had felt amazing to be in wolf form after years without when I'd arrived in Hell. But I hadn't shifted back since. She had her own whims, and that was scary for me, who'd always had so little control.

"So what do you suggest? I go for a run in the nearby area and let her catch some more rabbits?"

Cole snorted.

"You're a wolf shifter, not a normal hound." I wasn't sure what that meant because my wolf really had enjoyed chasing that rabbit down.

I couldn't have anticipated his next words.

"Fight me."

Cole didn't wait for my reaction, already heading to the large, padded area that could serve as a makeshift sparring ring.

"Cole, wait." I hurried to catch up.

He looked back as if to say, *What now?*

"I... I don't know if this is such a good idea."

"It's better than any of yours."

I exhaled through my nose, trying for patience. Goddess, this male frustrated me. And that was what worried me. I didn't have a lot of control over my wolf. She might take all my frustration with Cole and seriously come at him. "I might hurt you," I said.

At this, Cole actually did laugh.

"I'm serious!"

"Don't flatter yourself, little wolf."

I growled at his use of the nickname.

"Fine. If that's how you want it." It would serve him right if my wolf bit a chunk out of his torso.

Even if I knew it was a really good-looking torso. That was a sacrifice I was willing to make if it meant taking Cole down a peg. So what if I could barely lift a third of the weight he did? As a wolf, I had fangs and claws. They'd been close to the surface for days. It was time to let them out.

Now, I just needed to shift.

Which presented a bit of a problem. I didn't want to be left without clothing, and I didn't want to undress in front of Cole.

"Turn around," I told him.

He rolled his eyes. "It's nothing I haven't seen before."

Shifters were usually casual about nudity, but I had less experience with it than most. And... and it was *Cole*.

I crossed my arms over my chest and stared him down until he finally turned.

Okay. I quickly shucked off my clothes and set them in a pile.

Now to shift.

I expected to find it difficult, the way it had always been, but my wolf was right there. The second I willed it, my body transformed, bones breaking and restructuring. It was painful, but only in the way it was when you stretched a muscle after sitting too long.

Within moments, I was in my wolf form. I stared down at my front paws, flexing them, getting a feel for my body. My wolf, she was there too. More prominent. I raised my head, tasting the air. There were new dimensions, nuances only my wolf's nose could trace. One scent in particular, carried on the wind, excited my wolf.

Cole's.

Finally, I lowered my head, leveling my gaze on Cole. He'd turned back around and was staring at me. Perhaps it was my color. I'd never heard of another red wolf.

And then my wolf charged.

It was without thought, and I panicked, trying to regain control. But my wolf had effectively shut me out. She was running at Cole, and for all my bravado about biting his torso, I didn't actually want to maim my reluctant host.

Shit. Shit, shit, *shit*.

Cole didn't move. Didn't even tense. Twenty feet between us to start. Ten. Five. My wolf moved like the wind, fast, effortless, until she slammed into him.

Our bodies collided, and Cole went down without so much as a grunt.

Seriously, would it have killed him to dodge? I'd tried to

warn him!

But my wolf didn't immediately go for the jugular.

No, my wolf-side, the killer that lurked beneath my fur, she bent her head down to Cole's face...

And she licked him.

Um, hi, wolf-self, I tried to tell her. *Let's try that jugular thing instead.*

My wolf ignored me, continuing to lick Cole. The taste of his skin was embedded on my tongue, and I hated that even in my wolf form, I could tell I liked it. It was like his scent on steroids. I wanted it all over me. I wanted to rub myself in it. Wanted to roll around, to mix it with mine...

Okay, clearly the wolf's psyche was winning out over mine.

Cole raised his hand. I'd almost be grateful to him when he shoved me off because this was mortifying.

But when he raised his hand, he didn't use it to push me off. Instead, his hand came up, past my chest where I stood over him, and reached for my ear.

And then he scratched.

Holy cheeseballs. That felt good. Like so good. He eased out from under me, continuing to scratch.

Seriously. Avery Ward, Wolf Shifter Extraordinaire. I had the survival instincts of an overly friendly golden retriever.

He kept scratching, and part of me was mad at him. Like, okay, my wolf was rusty. Cole did smell and taste super good. There were no other shifters around, and maybe he was a little like a packmate. In the absolute barest sense of the word.

So she could be forgiven.

But he was petting me like I was a pet dog or something. What was up with that? Cole, Mr. I-overestimated-your-ability-to-survive, Sir Grouch himself was scratching my ear like a loyal lapdog.

I tried harder than ever to overpower my wolf's will. To make her move away from him.

She shifted on her feet. I felt a surge of hope that this humiliation would end and we could go back to sparring.

And then she flopped on her back, looking up at Cole expectantly.

He bent down over my exposed stomach and lifted a hand. I tried to glare at him from behind the wolf's eyes. *Don't you dare. Don't even think about it.*

But neither Cole nor the wolf gave a shit. He slowly stroked my stomach once, and I was in heaven, tongue loose, panting, eager for more. He continued to stroke, and for a moment, the sensation was so blissful, so overwhelming, it overshadowed any trace of remaining pride.

No, no, no, my human psyche yelled, fighting to resurface. *Do not let him pet you!* I kept yelling at my wolf, demanding to take control back.

She growled. Cole paused for a second, then continued.

Because she'd been growling at *me*. She wanted me to stop disrupting her—our—belly rub.

Would my humiliation never end?

From behind the wolf's eyes, I could make out Cole's face. The smirk on his lips.

"Not so dangerous after all," he mused.

I wanted to claw him. Instead, my tail twitched like it was going to wag.

Why was my wolf so shameless?

It took longer than I'd like to admit but, eventually, I wrangled control back. I couldn't win in wolf form, but I could shift back to my human shape.

Laying naked at Cole's feet was a different type of mortification. I sprinted over to my clothes, pulling them on as fast as I could.

"What the hell?" I hissed once there were ten feet between us and I was dressed.

My face was burning. Scratch that, my whole body was. Those good feelings from Cole rubbing my body hadn't gone away. No, they'd been translated to very human equivalents, and I was suddenly desperate for a cold shower.

Cole shrugged, looking utterly unbothered. Of course he was unbothered. He hadn't just involuntarily splayed himself in front of me with the wolfy-equivalent of a come-hither look.

"Guess you have more work to do."

Yeah. No shit.

CHAPTER XVI

COLE, WITHOUT ANY FURTHER discussion, appointed himself my trainer. He decreed that we would meet every morning to train so I didn't 'try and hump my enemies to death.' I'd wanted to claw his face off, but I was still mortified over the whole thing.

He at least offered me a reprieve a few days before next demanding I shift. Instead, he ordered me around the rooftop gym. Laps around the roof, weight-lifting, more sit-ups than I could stomach.

No wonder Cole's body looked the way he did if he worked out like this.

Though, I thought that wasn't quite right. His body wasn't made from a set regimen of exercises. It was honed through battle.

I'd had all too much time to contemplate his body while we worked out since he was often shirtless.

He'd caught me staring one day—I was just taking a breather, honest—and he'd given me the cockiest wink imaginable.

That was the duality of Cole. Sometimes I swore he almost hated my guts, he was so prickly around me. Every incorrect lift was critiqued, any stumble in my running earning a terse reprimand to pick up my damn feet.

But then he would do something like wink. And I'd swear it was his version of flirting before deciding I'd sweat so much I was dehydrated and, by extension, hallucinating.

In the privacy of my room, I did practice shifting. My wolf didn't enjoy being confined. The agitation made it that much harder to communicate between our two psyches, but I was unwilling to risk another embarrassing episode like before.

In the afternoon, I was free to explore the castle. Most of the time I was so exhausted I slept the day away—after devouring half the kitchen.

But not today. Today, something urged me to explore.

Cole disappeared in the afternoons, giving me some semblance of privacy. He had not, however, given me any type of tour. I could reliably find my way to the roof, and that was only because Cole got extra sadistic when he had to hunt me down from the labyrinth of the castle.

The halls were endless, the only landmarks were the statues in the corners. They gave me the willies with their eerily life-like expressions, but they were the only chance I stood of not getting hopelessly lost in this place every time I left my room.

For example, I got to the gym by heading down to the stone dog, then left at the snake lady, followed by a right at the giant spider perched on the wall until I hit the staircase.

I went a different way, wandering down corridors as if guided by some sixth sense. I didn't think I'd been in this part of the castle before, but it was honestly hard to tell since it all looked so similar. I reached the second floor and came to a massive double door.

I glanced around as if Cole was going to spring out of the shadows and tell me off for snooping.

Then again, he'd never said I couldn't explore. And since he was convinced I would be mincemeat the second I stepped outside the castle, it was only fair I get to explore inside.

I set my shoulders back and pushed the doors open.

My jaw dropped.

A library. But not like what I was used to—the only library the pack had was the one in school, and everything there was covered by a thin layer of dust and disinterest. Moon-Ghost hadn't really bred readers. Another way I hadn't fit in—I'd adored that little library, at least when I could escape there between classes for a few minutes.

No, that dusty old room and this... they didn't belong in the same sentence.

The castle's library was massive, with floor-to-ceiling shelves lining every wall, with a few stacks further dividing the room. All the way at the far end, there was a fire burning, with two seats in front of it.

For some reason, those seats were even more intriguing

than the books. I crossed the massive room, frowning.

Cole said the castle had its own kind of magic, providing different things as needed. But these chairs looked worn. Matching plush chairs with a shared table between them. A few books were stacked there, bookmarks inching out of the pages.

I scanned the spines. The History of War. Chemistry of Gemstones. Phytotoxicology.

Weird. Aside from the first, not what I would've guessed Cole liked to read.

Then again, it was hard to picture him here, curled up in a chair, relaxing in front of the fire. Cole hardly ever seemed to relax.

He looked pretty relaxed in that bed. The thought came before I could stop it.

Come to think of it, he hadn't found it weird that someone was in his bedroom. Not until he saw me. Was that a normal occurrence? It hadn't stood out to me at the time, but since the nixie, I hadn't seen another living soul.

I put the books back down and went over to the shelves.

The wealth of knowledge was overwhelming. Even if I had a thousand years, I wasn't sure it would be enough time to read everything here.

The topics varied widely. Politics, both of humans and the supernatural. Strategy books. Novels, none of which seemed familiar. Mythology from all denominations, from shifter beliefs to an entire shelf of Greek myths.

Maybe there was something here that would help me. A guide to the underworld. A few books proved promising, and I collected them in my arms. One was titled A Guide to the Realms. Another was about shifter transformation, which I hoped might have some useful clues for controlling my wolf. By the time I pulled a third off the shelf, a book on magical creatures, my arms were overfull. I was about to turn away when my attention snagged on one book in particular.

Portals.

A simple title to a hefty book. I pulled it from the shelf and went over to the fire for better light to read in.

There's a great deal of mysticism around portals, but in truth, they are like any other door. You walk in on one side, and you exit the other. The only difference is these two places need not be physically next to each other.

Odd. Not really relevant to anything, but interesting. I set it aside and went through my more practical selections. The magical creature encyclopedia informed me the blue creature I'd come across in the cave had been a Taurus demon, a subset of the demons that were native to Hell. Unlike the rest of the inhabitants. The book explained they were highly territorial and aggressive, if not very intelligent.

Would've been nice to know that a few days ago.

The shifter manual wasn't much use. It spent pages going on about inner peace and harmony and balance without any actionable advice, and I quickly grew bored of it.

The third book, the Guide to the Realms, was the most intriguing, but it was a dense read. Each page was filled with a dozen words I didn't know. Some were species which I cross-referenced in the supernatural encyclopedia. The continent wasn't even mentioned until several hundred pages in, and I barely understood what I read about my own realm for that. It was known for weak magic, which seemed odd since we did have shifters and several other creatures, even if I'd never met anything else. I knew there were witches, vampires, and, according to this book, demons sometimes escaped to the continent...

I frowned. If demons could escape to the continent, why couldn't I?

The Taurus demon probably wouldn't welcome me with open arms even if I could find that cave again, but this was Hell. There had to be others.

I scanned the encyclopedia. There were dozens of varieties of demons, and I had no clue which would be most inclined to help. Probably not from the goodness of their heart, but I'd worry about that later. The first thing was to find one and get it to agree to take me to the continent.

And I knew just the male to help me.

THERE WERE NO TWO ways about it. Cole was a sadist.

The morning started with laps. Those weren't so bad. My body was quickly gaining strength, and the miles I ran around the roof to start the day were a familiar warm-up.

Then Cole added obstacles. Still fine.

Then he moved me through a series of calisthenics that had my worn muscles screaming.

But the worst was the weights. Gone were the simple lifts we'd started with. My muscles screamed within minutes of following his commands. Pulse, lift, hold still. Drop, lift. Lean forward. Lift higher.

It was as mental as it was physical. Sometimes there would be minutes of endless silence save my grunts as I lifted the weights between commands, and my mind couldn't afford to wander in those seconds without strict reprimand.

All in all, it was torture. Mental and physical.

"Maybe we should go back to sparring." Thirst clawed at me. I choked down water from a bucket, dehydrated after all but sweating out of my skin.

Cole snorted. "Can't say I ever remember sparring in the first place."

I rolled my eyes. Was he ever going to let me live that humiliating episode down now? "I might surprise you."

Despite the grueling regimen, or because of it, I did sense a little progress. My sessions with my wolf in the room went better. I couldn't always wrest control from her, but sometimes she'd agree to take the backseat for a little. The shift was effortless. A part of me even now was dying to shed my human skin and let her feel the open air through her fur.

But I didn't really want to talk about that. Before he could inform me in that charming way of his that "break time was over, so stop standing around and get back to it" I blurted what was really on my mind.

"What do you know about meeting demons in Hell?"

Cole narrowed his gaze on me. "Why would you want anything to do with them?"

I shrugged, hoping for casual. I wasn't ready to tell him my plan yet. "I read in a book here that they're native to this realm. Shouldn't I familiarize myself with other people here?" Cole looked unconvinced. "I mean, a girl has to make friends somehow," I joked.

There was a grain of truth there, though. Not that I needed demon friends, but that I was lonely.

"You don't need any friends like that." The words were decisive. Conversation over.

Except this conversation was so not over. "How would you know?"

At that, he arched an infuriating brow. "Little wolf, the things I know fill libraries."

I had enough clarity to know he was using that infuriating nickname to distract me. It wasn't going to work. Cole was avoiding answering my questions, which meant I wanted answers that much more.

"How do I find them?" I asked, not giving up.

"These are dangerous questions," he warned me.

Dangerous, maybe, but necessary if they held the key—or even possibility—of freeing me from this realm. "The one I faced before wasn't so tough."

"Then you met a weak one," he said, his tone dismissive. "Count your blessings and get back to training."

"I've trained plenty," I countered. "And I'm only asking how to find them, it's not like I'm going to head out tonight in search of them."

"This isn't a path you can go down while you're weak, Avery." The use of my name said he was dead serious, but it just annoyed me.

"I'm not weak!"

He shook his head. "It's not a criticism. It's the truth. If you can't recognize that, you're more of a fool than I thought."

I growled. I'd vowed never to be weak again, to never run, but in Cole's eyes, that's exactly what he saw. Someone content to hide in a castle because the outside world was too dangerous.

"I said I'm not weak." I was a goddess-damned wolf shifter. I had fangs and claws, and I could use them.

Cole growled back, irritated. He rarely lost his cool, but I was pushing him in a way I hadn't in a while. I got under his skin as much as he got under mine, for whatever comfort that offered.

"Tell you what, little wolf. Pin me. When you can manage that, I'll tell you all you want to know about those hell-spawned creatures and anything else you want to know."

If that was how he wanted it...

Cole clearly hadn't been expecting me to launch myself at him the second he stopped speaking, but he recovered quickly, dodging my outstretched arm as it came inches from hitting its mark on his face.

We'd been training for hours, but the raw adrenaline of a challenge pumped in my veins, staving off the exhaustion.

I threw myself at him. I might not be experienced at grappling, but some things are instinctive. Cole is bigger and stronger, no question, but I was determined.

I wanted answers. I wanted to see Daphne again. To go home, even if I wasn't sure what that meant. Hope has had barely a day to bloom in my chest, but it's a vine circling my heart and demanding action.

Cole, however, wasn't so easy to catch. He dodged my moves with infuriating grace. I continued on the offensive, driving him back, aiming to catch him off-guard with a good swipe.

I was so focused on hitting him I let my guard down. And when Cole went on the offensive, I was entirely unprepared.

In one swift movement, he took me off balance. Another sweep of my legs and I fell, crashing onto the padded floor.

Padded, yes, but with hard stone underneath. I gasped, drawing for air. Having the wind knocked out of me sucks, but Cole wasn't done. He pulled himself down on top of me. One thick thigh pinned my legs, and in the same movement, he captured my wrists with one hand, pinning them above my head.

Shit.

CHAPTER XVII

COLE PINNED ME IN place, leaning over. One hand held my wrists in a vise above my head, the other braced next to my head. His scent was all around me. I couldn't help but inhale it, taste it on my tongue with rapid, shallow breaths.

Masculine. Powerful.

Alpha.

It radiated off of him, making me want to submit. From my place on the floor, he was almost a giant. I was forced to look up at him. He'd pinned me. Before this, he'd been playing with me. There was no way I could beat him.

No. I refused to give in. I needed answers. I tried to shake him off, not willing to concede. I nearly dislocated my shoulder trying to pull a hand loose from his grip, shifting under him, trying to dislodge his thigh that pinned me to the mat.

Cole didn't budge. He leaned closer until his head was mere inches from mine as he leaned over me.

"Foreplay won't win you battles."

My eyes went wide as I immediately became aware of the

way our bodies were touching. The way I'd been wriggling against him.

The way a very, very large bulge was pressed against my pelvis.

I went utterly still, audibly swallowing.

Cole just arched a cool brow as if to say, *You brought this on yourself.*

He was close. To make matters worse, I was training only in a pair of leggings and cropped tank top. Cole was shirtless, that mysterious tattoo on display. The one that went all the way down and made me constantly want to see the edges of it.

"If this is foreplay, then your version of sex is probably getting stabbed," I stammered, trying to think of a witty comeback that would divert the attention from his hard member pressing against me. And the way my body was reacting to it.

"Oh, I'm usually the one doing the 'stabbing.' Do you need a demonstration of that too?"

I sputtered, flustered by his words. Cole could flip from brutal to downright sensual at the drop of a hat, and I was pretty sure if he was going to pin me, I'd rather him be brutally attacking me. It was easier to handle having my ass kicked than whatever I was feeling right now.

My skin was electrified. Something sparked under it. The urge to throw him off.

The urge to climb on top of him.

"Can you get off of me?" I demanded.

Cole didn't relax his grip at all. "Submit."

"You've got me pinned, and clearly I can't toss you on your ass"—yet—"so isn't that enough?"

He bared his teeth, the sensuality of the previous moment gone. "Submit."

Fine. If that's what it would take to get him off me.

I lifted my chin in reluctant submission. I hated the vulnerability of the movement, the admission of defeat.

It was more than that. Submitting like this... it went beyond sparring. But nothing less would satisfy Cole, apparently.

My wolf growled inside, disliking the demand. *So now you're mad and want to fight him? Maybe if you worked with me, we would've won.* The point was moot for now. It would be a while before I could defeat Cole, if ever.

Though I hadn't seen Cole shift since that day I'd nearly been drowned by the nixie, instinctively I knew he and his wolf were in sync. Even when he was in the shape of a man, the wolf prowled under the surface. It would take me years to reach that equilibrium. I doubted the pack alphas I'd met could match him.

No, winning with brute strength would take too long. I'd need to find another way to get answers.

"Even as you submit, you seem more resolved than ever." There was an odd undercurrent to the words. Not his usual abrasiveness or flirtation. Something almost somber echoed in them. Finally, his grip loosened slightly, though he didn't move away immediately.

Instead, he looked down at me. His face was still mere inches from mine. He had the slightest stubble. If I arched, lifted myself, we'd be able to touch.

I almost demanded he get off again, but what kept me frozen was the expression in his eyes. Not triumph, not dominance.

No, a hazy emotion. Something closer to... longing, I realized with surprise.

As quickly as the realization came, Cole was off of me, jumping up in one smooth movement and suddenly halfway across the castle roof. I half wondered if I'd imagined it. But I knew I hadn't.

Then again, of course, Cole was lonely. He was a wolf without a pack. Somewhere along the way, I'd started to think of him as almost a member of mine, but that was probably a mistake. There was no way he'd consider me one of his. At best, he thought of me as some wayward pet.

Still, he'd helped me. Even with the humiliation of my submission clinging to my skin—really, as an Omega, I shouldn't have had such a hard time with it, but my wolf loathed it—I was grateful.

It was hard to keep track of time in the realm, but it had been at least a month since Cole had started to train me, and

I could feel a difference.

Maybe I should tell him. A calculating part of me hoped it might soften him slightly and maybe make him willing to tell me what I wanted to know.

But deep down, the truth was, I just wanted him to know.

He stood at the edge of the castle roof, staring off in the distance. He didn't turn his head, even as he heard me approach. I lifted myself onto the merlon, following his gaze into the distance.

The light was fading. The moat of lava that circled the castle brightened our immediate area. From this side of the castle, we didn't face the river but the direction I'd originally come from.

For several minutes, there was only silence. It wasn't entirely bad. In a way I was reluctant to admit, it reminded me of the evenings I'd spent with Daphne, hanging out on a random roof, stargazing. She would try and identify her ancestors in the sky, where the Moon Goddess had placed them. I'd never been able to join in.

It made sense, I suppose. I hadn't been placed among the stars, after all. I'd been given a one-way ticket to Hell.

I might've sat there in silence all night, but I'd come over to say something specific. I cleared my throat slightly, forcing the words out. Gratitude never came easy for me, partly because I'd never had much to be thankful for.

"Thank you for training me," I said quickly.

There. The silence was broken.

Cole's gaze slid to me. I didn't have to look at him to know he was giving me a skeptical look. "Did you hit your head too hard when I flipped you?"

I rolled my eyes at him. "You enjoyed that too much."

Cole made a noise in his throat, slipping a rough note into his next words. "I think I enjoyed it just the right amount."

Innuendo obvious, my mind involuntarily went back to that moment, with his body pressed against mine. I'd only been referring to him knocking me down. My wolf, who I was trying to pay more attention to, was undecided. She'd enjoyed the proximity and despised the submission. "You're such an ass," I grumbled.

"Ah, gratitude. So fleeting," Cole said sarcastically. "Admit it, you came over here to try and convince me to tell you the answers you failed to earn."

Okay, maybe that was partly true. "I *am* grateful," I insisted. "For you training me these past few weeks. I feel stronger. More in sync with her."

"Her?" he queried.

"My wolf," I clarified.

"You think of your wolf as a separate entity." A statement, not a question, but I frowned.

"I mean, isn't that the whole deal? Shifters have two spirits, the wolf and the human." Or something like that.

Cole's lips twisted in contempt. "Is that what they're

teaching pups these days?"

Now I frowned. "You're saying we're really one spirit? Then why does my wolf want—" I shut my mouth before I brought up my wolf's constant desire to have Cole pet her fur and scratch her under the chin. It was mortifying.

Cole gave me a look that said he knew exactly what I was going to say, but generously would ignore that elephant in the room. "You're one creature. In the same way you can have two different thoughts at the same time, your human side and wolf side may disagree on occasion. But it's not you and your wolf side, where the human side is the true you. You're one entity with the ability to shift forms as needed." I nodded, trying to take in what he was saying. Was I making this harder on myself by going against my wolf side? But then again, she—I?—didn't behave. How could I solve that? "Or you will be once you gain some fucking control," he added.

I growled at the reminder. Cole snapped his teeth at me, a warning that his wolf side was very present. I was tempted to hiss, but that just wouldn't be dignified.

"How come you'll answer these questions but not the other ones?" I asked.

A wary look. "Why won't you stop asking questions that will get you killed?"

"I don't see what favor ignorance ever did anyone," I snapped. "Like the nixie. If I'd *known* about it, I wouldn't have almost drowned."

"If you'd just kept walking, you wouldn't have almost gotten your ass thrown in Tartarus, either," Cole snapped back with heat. Bringing the nixie up was probably a bad move. He seemed to get downright pissed whenever I mentioned that day by the river. "Why are you even so invested in getting back? If it got you killed, I can't imagine there's any real prize there."

"Maybe I want to get back to my moon-matched mate," I deflected. Truth was, there wasn't really anything for me back in Moon-Ghost. Except for Daphne. Was she okay? Did she know what had happened?

And I wouldn't mind kicking Jett's teeth in. Just the thought made me want to growl.

But it was Cole who snarled. A low, dangerous sound that made me shift uneasily. What, he didn't like me talking about my mate?

Cole saw the look I gave him and the throaty sound cut off immediately like he'd just remembered himself. "If that mate was worth a damn, he would've protected you from whatever killed you."

Or wouldn't have had me killed. It was on the tip of my tongue to clarify for Cole, but why would I? He'd never asked about the circumstances of my death, and I wasn't going to make myself look any more pathetic in his eyes if I could help it.

Forsaken by my own mate. Could I sink any lower?

I didn't let myself consider the alternative—actually living my life as the Alpha heir's mate. That would've been a different Hell.

"Anyway, my reasons don't matter," I said, redirecting the conversation. "All I'm asking is for you to tell me where I would find the demons."

"There's no point," Cole said, dismissing me. "You won't be killed so long as you're staying at the castle."

Frustration gnawed at me. "I can't stay here forever."

"Why not?" he shot back. "You have all the food you can eat. A place to sleep. You're safe here."

"It might not always be safe. I mean, you keep pointing out that this is Hell. What if, I don't know, demons attack it? Or nixies. Or whatever else crawls around this realm that you won't tell me about."

Cole snorted like the idea was preposterous. "No one would dare attack the castle."

I rolled my eyes at his cavalier dismissal. "Right, because you're so all-powerful they're too scared to make a move."

"Exactly." The sheer arrogance of his agreement rankled. The male had a high opinion of himself, and maybe somewhat deserved, but he was just a shifter, like me.

A bit—okay, a lot—stronger than me, but still.

"And what happens if you get sick of me? You barely let me stay one night before kicking me out, after all. What if you decide to do that again?"

Cole was silent at that. He didn't say anything, didn't protest the way I described what he'd done, didn't claim he'd never do that again.

I hadn't really expected him to. It would be out of character for him to plead like that, but it stung all the same. Like a thorn in my paw that I'd forgotten was there until I'd pressed on it.

"That's what I thought." I swung around off my perch and marched to the other side of the roof. Cole didn't move. As I turned to take the stairs down, he was still looking away in the distance, not sparing so much as a backward glance for me.

Fuck him. I didn't need Cole's help. One way or another, I was going to find a way out of Hell.

CHAPTER XVIII

G ETTING COLE TO ANSWER my questions had proved futile, but that didn't mean I was giving up. I spent almost every waking moment not training reading book after book. The library held the answers, I was certain. If I could just find them.

I'd curl up in one of the worn chairs for hours in the evening. On rare occasions, Cole would also find his way to the library. He never took the seat next to me, the single other chair. Instead, he'd browse the shelves—sometimes for minutes. Others, hours—and then leave. We didn't speak. It pissed me off that he wouldn't answer questions about most things I read, so I quit asking.

The books were informative, but it wasn't like there was one called *How to Get Out of Hell in Three Easy Steps*. I didn't even know what I was looking for. I'd read the one on portals cover to cover, and unfortunately, it hadn't been too helpful. It was mostly generic, metaphorical crap.

The most concrete things I'd learned: demons definitely controlled the portals in Hell, and not just any demon, but a specific type, Libra demons. There were no tips on how to identify them from others. Just that they tended to hang out in the cities of Hell. Of course, there were no maps for me to reference or names of cities I could search for. When I'd desperately asked Cole one day, he'd arched one infuriating brow and asked mildly, "Are you *trying* to die again?"

Sometimes, when I got bored, I read through different mythology collections. Just to take my mind off of my situation. In some ways, Cole did have a point. Why did I want to go back? My life in Moon-Ghost had been more hellish than, well, Hell.

But I wasn't built to sit around. I needed a purpose. For years, it had been simply to survive. But no longer would I settle, resign myself to being a passive little wolf pup. I needed a goal to work towards, to focus me.

Cole would argue my goal really should be to be a better shifter. I was not living up to his expectations, even with the countless hours of training each week.

I continued to spar with him every few days, even if I knew logically it wasn't ever going to yield to answers I needed. But my wolf—or what I'd been thinking of as my wolf—wanted it. I kept indulging the urge. Maybe a little more give and take might help us reach equilibrium. Maybe I'd unite both sides with the bloodthirsty need to dominate Cole, to defeat him.

Unfortunately, I was starting to suspect my wolf side just really enjoyed being pinned by Cole.

Cole, displeased with my progress, had started to get creative in his training.

And Cole's creativity was a thing to be very afraid of.

Today's activity? Apparently, Cole was sick of me constantly getting lost in this enormous castle and had instructed me to find and map out a list of specific statues.

I wrinkled my nose as he held the parchment out to me. "What? Don't think you're up for it?" he taunted.

I snatched the paper and scanned the list. "I just don't see what good finding a twelve-leg octopus—which that kind of goes against the 'octo' part of octopus—and a hippal… hippalectrocute—"

"Hippalectryon," Cole corrected. "It's half horse, half rooster."

He had that way about him like these things should be obvious, because he was used to having all the answers. It drove me nuts when we were training.

He'd met me outside my room this morning and informed me that we wouldn't be bothering with the roof today. Consequently, he wasn't in his usual workout gear. Instead, he wore more formal clothes. Black slacks, a deep indigo shirt that looked like silk. Oddly, it seemed to suit him just as well as the casual gear he'd been wearing as of late. It reminded me of what I'd seen him in the first day we'd met.

We didn't match at all since I'd expected to be training. I was in a cropped pair of leggings and a loose sweatshirt over a sports bra. Normally, I'd be thrilled with my ensemble, but for some reason, it felt odd this morning.

"Whatever. I don't see what any of these have to do with reaching that state of equilibrium you talk about."

"Of course you don't," Cole said. "That's why I'm the teacher, and you do what you're told."

Cole thought I was some obedient little student who did as instructed? He must be thinking of someone else...

Though suddenly, I imagined myself in a schoolgirl uniform and Cole in a suit, just like the one he currently wore, and maybe a ruler...

Cole let out an exasperated sigh. "Would you just listen?" Apparently, I'd missed what he'd just said. Whoops. His jaw was doing that twitchy thing it did when I really got on his nerves. I pushed the daydream away—and I did *not* want to daydream about Cole anyway, it wasn't my fault he was the only male around—and forced myself to listen. "You should learn to identify them by scent only and be able to find your way through the castle with no issue. You have until the end of the day to do it."

I let out an exasperated huff. "What do you mean, they smell different? The statues are all made from the same stone, aren't they?"

He leveled me with a look. "Trust your wolf senses. You'll detect nuances of the base creature you weren't bothering to notice before."

Base creature? "They *are* just statues, right?" I glanced to the one at the end of the hall on my right. It was a little cupid-looking thing if Cupid was about two hundred pounds. "It's not like they're *alive...*"

"Which reminds me," Cole said, completely ignoring my question, "don't go to the underground level. Mapping the main two floors will be sufficient."

"Why? Is that where your sex dungeon is?"

Holy shit, what had just come out of my mouth? Seriously, one comment and I'm picturing a little teacher roleplay, and the next I'm thinking about sex dungeons.

Maybe this is my real Hell. Intrusive dirty thoughts about Cole.

"No, just my normal dungeon," Cole deadpanned. But I didn't miss the way the corners of his lips twitched like he wanted to laugh. Or smirk. He did a lot of smirking.

My mortification faded as I continued to eye the fat, winged baby at the end of the hall. "Cole, the statues aren't actually alive, right?"

"As they say, Hell hath no fury like a woman scorned," he said, once again not answering my question. I was starting to worry that was the answer. He turned away, off to who knows where. "Just find the statues on the list. There'll be a quiz."

And I was thinking about a ruler again.

I read through the list. Half a dozen statues of various descriptions to single out, but if my guess was accurate after the weeks I'd been here, there were hundreds to find. The first one on the list, a mermaid, I actually remembered seeing, if only because it was by the kitchen. That would be my first stop, with the added benefit of letting me grab some breakfast.

Once my stomach was satisfied, I eyed the mermaid. It was shorter than me, partly because the tail was curled. I approached with caution like it would move at any moment.

It's just a statue, I repeated over and over in my head. *Just a statue.*

I leaned closer and sniffed. *See? Just stone.*

I was ready to dart off in search of the next marble chunk on my list, but something teased at my senses. I eyed the statue again. There was something else to the scent. In my normal state, I couldn't detect it. But I wasn't a normal person, I was a shifter. Enhanced senses were my birthright. I paused, trying to draw on Cole's many lessons about reaching equilibrium with my wolf side. I'd felt it, sometimes, sparring against Cole. More in sync with myself. But I couldn't summon that concentration on command, and I couldn't maintain it. It was like the two sides of me kept warring when I was training with him.

But I should be able to draw on my enhanced senses by now. I shut my eyes for focus, trying to summon the wolf side of me forward.

My fingers twitched with the urge to give in to the wolf. No matter how Cole said we were on the same, it was hard not to think of my wolf side as another entity. The urge to change shapes, to give in, was seductive. It was so freeing to be in that form. To take the backseat and let my inner animal do as she pleased.

No. I didn't want to shift. I just wanted to draw on a small portion of that power.

My hearing sharpened first. The crackle of the torches that lined the hall was sharper. Then, scent. The fresh brownies from the kitchen wafted over, more potent than before.

Got it. I leaned in, inhaling once more with my newly sharpened sense of smell.

Stone. Still stone, hints of earthiness.

But there was more. Under it. Almost fishy. Saltwater.

My eyes snapped open, and I jumped back from the statue.

Holy shit, this was a real mermaid.

I poked the statue once, then twice, watching for any movement. But her stone-carved expression didn't shift.

I started to walk off. Counted ten paces. Then I spun around and darted back to the statue.

Still no movement.

One more knock against the statue, which made my knuckles hurt. Nope. This was definitely a statue.

But it had been a living creature first.

CHAPTER XIX

HOLY SWEET CHEESE NUGGETS, did this mean *all* the statues were real creatures?

Probably. It explained why Cole had tasked me with sniffing them all. There wouldn't be any way to tell them all apart without that extra sense.

It put my task in a new light. I tried on the next three statues, and each, under the base layer of stone, smelled different. I took my time examining them. They weren't simply artistic sculptures but different creatures. I'd known there were more than shifters and humans on the continent. Witches, demons, and vampires, to name a few. But cloistered in Moon-Ghost without an opportunity to explore, I'd never met anyone who wasn't a shifter. Until the night of the Choosing, I'd never even met someone who wasn't in the pack.

I continued to roam the halls. The different scents actually did help my internal map, like a puzzle piece clicking into place. I'd been trying to learn the routes before, but this made it easier. Not easy, of course. No task Cole assigned could be called easy. It took me three laps of the first floor to confidently map out the space. By that point, I was almost dizzy. About half the items on the list remained, including the mister rooster-horse. Time to try the second floor.

My explorations of the second floor were mainly limited to the library, so that was my starting point. I shot the double doors a wistful look as I passed by, wishing I could just curl up in one of the worn armchairs with a book.

But I wasn't about to quit. Instead, I explored just about every crevice of the second floor, testing my newly forced mental map as I went. Another two hours later, I was exhausted. My wolf side was getting tired of sniffing statues, and I couldn't blame her. Me. Whatever. Those things had been creepy to begin with, and now that I knew they were real?

I was going to give Cole *so* much shit for this.

First, I needed to find him. It was hard to gauge the time from inside the castle. His bedroom door had been shut each time I'd walked by, the room silent, and I hadn't seen him since he'd issued his orders. He might have been on the roof, which would be the most logical place to check, except he wasn't usually there unless he was training.

How strange to live in the same castle as a male for weeks and not be sure where he hung out during the day.

But I was a wolf. And I'd hunt him down if that was what it took.

I retraced my steps on the second floor, then paused at a hallway I didn't recognize. It was impossible to trace every hallway in a single day. I must've missed this one on my earlier pass-through.

I walked down the hall, casting my enhanced hearing out for any sign of Cole.

Then, I heard a familiar, low timbre.

I took a step forward, then paused. Who was Cole talking to? I hadn't seen another person since the nixie in the river.

I crept closer to the source of the sound before landing at a shut door.

"I don't care where you send them, just take care of them. I'm busy."

"You should visit sometime. You're missed," a soft, lilting voice chastised.

Who is that? There was something overly familiar in that feminine voice that pissed me off. A growl rose in my throat, and I had to slap my hands over my mouth to hold it back. *What the Hell, wolf side, don't sell us out.*

Cole didn't reply for a moment.

"Everything okay?" the female voice asked.

I didn't even breathe for fear of discovery. I did not want to see Cole's reaction to my snooping on him.

But I was curious, and that fear wasn't enough to send me running from my crouched position outside the door.

"It was nothing," Cole said after a moment, and I quietly exhaled a sigh of relief.

"The souls need attention," the voice continued, tenderly

prodding Cole in a way that made me grind my teeth. "There have been several applications for reincarnation, and at least one holds merit."

Reincarnation? Like coming back from the dead? And who was this woman? Cole had said it was just us in the castle, but last time I checked, there weren't cellphones in Hell.

"They can wait," Cole growled in his do-not-fuck-with-me voice.

It normally just made me want to argue. But the female simply said, "Of course, my lord."

Maybe that's how he likes his women. Submissive. Bent to his will. *Prick.* Jealousy stabbed me, and for the life of me, I couldn't figure out why. I had no claim to Cole. He didn't want me. Shit, the one male in the universe I had a claim to, my fated mate, didn't want me. I was altogether undesirable.

All the more reason to get back to Daphne. The one person who had ever wanted me for a packmate.

"But they cannot wait forever. The dead are restless."

"Are they?" Cole let out a dry chuckle. "Of course they are. They've been for millennia. Now is no different."

"Isn't it? You've not left your throne empty for this long before."

Cole growled, and his foots echoed through the stone like he was pacing. I wanted to hang around and sneak a peek at whoever he was talking to, but there was no sign of another person besides the voice. No footsteps, shifting feet, movement of the voice's source. *They must be communicating some way*, I decided. And I didn't want to be out in the hallway when Cole stopped pacing and stormed through the door.

I stood from my position and fled silently down the hall, turning over the conversation in my head. His throne? Cole did live in a castle, but I'd seen no sign of it. Reincarnation? Restless souls?

There was more to my reluctant roommate than met the eye.

WHEN COLE ASKED ME to show him the location of each statue the next day, I was proud of how quickly and accurately I managed to do so.

Cole was less impressed, the only acknowledgment a grudging nod of approval. Apparently, he wasn't impressed with the fact I'd been able to find my way to the kitchen without a single wrong turn this morning.

"Back to sparring then?" I asked cheerfully. Wandering the castle for hours, sniffing creepy, semi-living statues had not been my idea of a good time and I was not looking for a repeat.

I hadn't confronted Cole about the weird conversation yesterday. I debated just bluntly asking who he'd been talking to, but more likely he'd just chew me out for snooping. I'd come to learn when Cole didn't want to answer a question, he simply wouldn't. No amount of cajoling would change his mind. It vexed me to no end, even if it didn't always stop me from nagging him.

There was a lot I still didn't understand. Souls? Reincarnation? Cole's throne?

That had been an abrupt reminder this realm didn't exist within the same bounds as the continent. It was easy to forget this was the actual afterlife. I'd probably never learn all the rules, but if I could find a way out, it wouldn't matter, would it?

"In your dreams," Cole drawled. "I suppose you see me there often enough."

I flushed, then shook my head. "You wish," I said, unable to come up with anything better. My dreams had been surprisingly quiet for the past few weeks, and Cole had certainly not been present in them.

My thoughts the few minutes before sleep... I couldn't say the same. But I'd rather die (again) than admit that.

At least if he was in a teasing mood, he might take it easy on my training.

That turned out to be an extremely naive thought.

We didn't go to the roof. Instead, Cole led me down a hallway adorned with three unique monkey statues to a steel door.

"You need some pressure," Cole said, flirtation gone.

I glanced at the door. We'd clearly reached the place Cole

wanted to train today. Why wasn't he opening it?

"Pressure?" I echoed.

Cole nodded, a superior tilt of his head telling me I was not going to enjoy the impending lecture on how to be a better shifter, even if deep down I could admit he was right. "I've given you ample opportunity to bring both sides together, and I'm beginning to suspect you're the type who works better with some... motivation. Now's as good a time as any to test that theory."

What's behind the door? "What aren't you telling me?" I asked, suspicious.

Cole narrowed his eyes for a second, as if surprised I was calling him on his evasive bullshit. Then the look was gone like he didn't have a care in the world. "This is going to suck for you."

And then Cole opened the door.

A sense of wrongness hit me immediately. The space was almost completely empty, just another stone room like any other. Except for a large metal box in the middle of it, maybe four feet by four feet.

I had to consciously force myself not to take a step back.

"What is that?" I hissed. If Cole's goal was to unify my wolf side with the human he may have succeeded, because both parts of me agreed they did not like the box.

"Silver," was his one-word reply, like that explained everything. He stepped into the room like it was the most natural thing in the world. Did his shifter instincts not also tell him to get as far away as possible? Or, more likely, he'd mastered any pathetic reflexes ages ago.

"Why does it make me feel like this?" I asked. It was a monumental effort to force my way into the room. Not a physical block, but mentally, everything inside wanted to turn tail.

Cole frowned, looking back at me. "Don't tell me you don't know how silver affects shifters." The disapproval laced in his tone made me want to shrink almost as much as the silver itself.

"Can't say I've ever had the pleasure of coming across it," I said, trying to sound nonchalant. I'd wear any shred of bravado as armor.

Cole cursed with an abruptness that surprised me. "For fuck's sake, does your imbecile of an Alpha think if you don't know about your weaknesses, they won't exist?"

Probably. Maddox wasn't the type to expose any of his weaknesses. From my position as the pack punching bag for twenty years, he'd been a terrifying, all-powerful alpha. "I take it silver is harmful to us?"

"Simply, yes. Touching silver is unpleasant, which is why your instincts urge you *not* to. Of course, if you learn to stomach it, that makes silver weapons one of the best weapons you can use to kill a shifter. What happens if you're cut with a normal knife?" Professor Cole was in the mood for a pop quiz, apparently.

"It heals in a minute or two."

"Exactly. But a cut from a silver blade? You'll heal as slowly as a human. Ingesting it is as good as drinking arsenic."

Holy shit. How had I never known about this? Did all shifters know? Did they just hide it from the pups, or was Maddox hiding this from all of Moon-Ghost? He kept an iron grip on our ability to talk to the outside. As far as I knew, aside from minimal supply trades, the only interaction came from the annual gathering between the Fangs and Wind-Bloods at the Choosing.

My gaze flicked to the box. It wasn't completely solid metal, a few holes were cut into the top and sides.

Air holes, I realized after a beat.

"Don't tell me you're going to say today's task is going into that cage."

Cole's answering look was all the confirmation I needed.

"No way," I said immediately. "Absolutely not."

Memories of my days at the pack school flashed in my mind. *Not again.* Of all the torments I'd faced, the ones that left me claustrophobic were the worst.

"Scared?" The male arched a mocking brow. "Going to run with your tail between your legs?"

I straightened my spine. How dare he? I wasn't a coward, not anymore. But this cage... "How is this going to help me? My wolf and I both agree that thing is a torture device." Even now, my skin itched, like my wolf was ready to burst forward and flee on four legs if I wasn't capable of doing it on two.

"You're not separate creatures," Cole reminded me on reflex. He took a step towards me since I hadn't moved past the doorway. I bristled, expecting more goading or a lecture on how I was a crap shifter.

But Cole didn't do either of those things. Instead, he held my gaze for a moment. I stopped looking at the cage and let it steady me in a way I couldn't even understand.

"Avery, I'm not trying to fuck you over. Your wolf side isn't sensing any real danger when we spar"—no shit, since she kept trying to lick him—"and you aren't harmonizing the way you need to. You need some type of pressure, and I think this might help. Do you trust me to help you?"

I hesitated, then nodded. There might be a lot about Cole I didn't know or understand, but deep down, I trusted him with this.

"Then will you try this? If it works, this would probably be the fastest way to do it."

I shifted my weight back and forth on my feet. I didn't want Cole to think I was a quitter. That I was scared. And I desperately wanted to be a strong shifter. "Okay. Fine. What exactly am I supposed to do inside there?"

"Get out. Normally, shifters are nearly powerless against silver. But if you concentrate and truly reach equilibrium, you can force the box to bend as any other metal would."

I thought back to the barbell, which had my bench press maxing at two hundred pounds. Even if the cage was "any other metal" I wasn't sure I could bend it, but I had to believe Cole wouldn't set me up to fail.

"Okay, I'll do it," I repeated.

Cole nodded, a single movement of approval that bolstered my courage. He crossed the space to the cage in a few long strides while I forced myself to follow him. He unlatched one side, which I guess served as the door, and held it open to me. I'd clocked just the slightest flinch as he made contact but no other sign of discomfort.

Up close, somehow the cage looked even smaller. Fuck, did I hate small spaces.

"You're not going to lock me in there and leave?" I confirmed.

"I'll be here the whole time," he assured me.

I bent down and got inside the cage.

Cole shut the door behind me.

CHAPTER XX

T HE BOX WAS A thousand times worse now that I was standing inside it, surrounded on every side by silver. *Take a breath. You're okay.*

It was suffocating. I felt like I was choking, hunched over as I tried to get my bearings in the dark. It was too small for me to stand up, so I had to hunch down.

Inside, I was howling my distaste. *Focus,* I urged myself. But all I could do was feel the small space closing in on me.

Fuck. I'd spent more time than I'd ever wanted in small, enclosed spaces, and being caged again sent those memories flying around my head. I tried to steady myself, pressing a hand to the side before thinking better of it. I yelped from the contact. How was I ever going to get out of this? There was no way out. I couldn't touch the walls, let alone bend them.

I'm in over my head.

"Breathe, little wolf." Cole's voice felt so far away. Distant.

I tried to hold on to the words, but they were miles from me. The walls, on the other hand, were so close. So damn close.

Come on, wolf, harmonize and let's get out of here. But it felt farther away than ever.

Shit. Shit, shit, shit.

I had no space. I was trapped. There was no way out. No way out! I gave a desperate slam against the cage. There was no sense to the move, just a frantic need to get out.

But the silver wall didn't budge. I was weak. Pathetic. Like a mortal.

Like the Omega I'd been, shoved in lockers and out of the way. Forgotten. Forsaken.

My shoulder burned. I felt like I was going to pass out.

Fuck. I was trapped.

Small spaces. Hated small spaces. Hated being trapped.

I slammed at the wall again. Tears sprang to my eyes as pain ricocheted through my body.

Trapped.

I sunk down to the floor, clawing at my throat. I couldn't breathe. Couldn't breathe.

Not again. Please, not again, not again. The words slammed through my head, drowning out everything in the outside world. There was only darkness and suffocating silver and the blurriness in my head...

BAM!

Light. Air. The sudden change barely permeated through the fog. I registered a pair of hands pulling me out, taking me out of the cage. Pulling me into an embrace. Lifting me.

Moving me. I couldn't tell where. All I could do was continue to taste the silver.

Weak. I was weak. *Pathetic. Useless. Trapped.* The words spun up and down through my head, a Ferris wheel I couldn't escape.

"You're okay, little wolf." The voice was comforting. Familiar. *Mine.* But it all was caught up in the haze. I could see what was around me, but it felt like I was still inside, suffocating from the silver cage. "You're having a panic attack." The words were surprisingly gentle. "Focus. You're not trapped."

Not trapped. Slowly, the panic receded, leaving me panting, shaky breaths. I grew more aware of my surroundings. We weren't even in the same room anymore. Cole had taken me back to my own room. I blinked, stunned I'd somehow missed the part where we'd left. I'd never felt like that, never receded that way.

"Is it always like that?" I didn't recognize my voice. It was ragged, those few words tasting like glass shards.

"No." The word was quiet. "It's not. It's unpleasant, yes. Could drive a shifter mad if they're trapped there for days, weeks perhaps, but never like that."

Weakling. "I'm pathetic." And for Cole to see me that way... It was devastating for reasons I couldn't even name.

"*No.*" This time, the word was forceful. "You're not. You're strong. Trust yourself, Avery."

I belatedly realized I was clinging to Cole, my fists clenched to his shirt, but I couldn't bring myself to release the grip. I needed closeness. Touch. Any reminder that I wasn't trapped, alone, forgotten.

This close, I could drown myself in his scent. It was familiar to me, after living in the same castle for so long, but it wasn't often I could breathe it in directly like this.

"How can you say that?" My voice was soft, trying to maneuver the words around the scratchiness in my throat.

"Because I know you." A beat of silence. "What made you react like that? That was more than a shifter experiencing silver for the first time."

My breath hitched. *Not again. Someone, let me out!*

"Tell me." A command, but not a cruel one. Just enough to urge me to put those memories into words.

"I... I don't like small spaces," I confessed. "In my old pack, I was an Omega. And they bullied me for it. At first, it wasn't so bad. Maybe I was just slow at coming into my shifter powers. But by the time we hit middle school, it was obvious. I was the runt of our class. The weakest. The first day of middle school, the Alpha clique tossed me in a locker."

That day had been significant for two reasons. First, it brought me to my best friend, Daphne, since it was her locker I'd been shoved in. And it had also been the first time I'd dreamed of the voice. It had been different that first time. There'd been a body, a teasing glint in the eye of the figure, though it was all so hazy now. But that was just something I'd invented to comfort myself.

"But that wasn't the worst. I was found soon after. It didn't stop there. It seemed like I'd constantly be thrown in a locker between classes. The teachers refused to interfere, saying we had to sort out our pecking order ourselves. Really, it was just because the alpha's son was part of the group bullying me." A cruel but critical lesson: alphas can do whatever the fuck they want, and no one will help you. "Sometimes they'd hide me in other places. The gym storage closet... they barricaded me in on a Friday. No one found me until Monday."

"Your guardians didn't notice?" A sharp note of disapproval.

I snorted. My mother? If I wasn't home for a weekend, she was probably just thanking her good fortune. "The worst was the trunk. I think that's what made me freak out. They ambushed me after school and took me to the woods. They forced me to go inside a trunk. Smaller than the cave of silver, but it didn't have air holes. They locked it shut and then they had their fun." Name-calling, which shouldn't have hurt by that point. *We should just bury the garbage,* Sabine had crowed. Kicking it. Knocking the trunk over again and again until I was dizzy and bruised. "The only reason I didn't suffocate was I managed to shift a single finger to a claw and cut a hole in the side. My friend found me hours later." Daphne had been furious, but what was there to do? I was an outcast in every way.

Cole was motionless beside me. I glanced up at him, afraid of what he'd think. Since I'd come to Hell, I hadn't thought of myself as that weak little pup, the Alpha clique's whipping toy. I'd been able to shift. I'd learned to fight. I'd gotten stronger.

But back in that cage, I'd felt every bit the runt I'd been in Moon-Ghost.

Cole's face was a mask. Normally, I had some inkling of what he was thinking, but now I couldn't begin to guess.

"I ran after that," I admitted. "When I saw them coming, I'd turn the other way. They rarely managed to get the jump on me after that." Self-loathing filled me. Wolves were supposed to stand their ground and fight for their place in the pack. Not turn tail.

But how could I win when they constantly ganged up on me?

"Who were they?" A simple question. Probably to take my mind off of it.

"I called them the Alpha clique," I explained. "Sabine was the worst. She was always angling to be the alpha's mate. Richard was the muscle, jumping to follow her orders, and then there was Jett." I hated that I choked on the name, that I turned away from Cole as pain stabbed me at the memory of the alpha's son. "He was the Moon-Ghost heir. And my moon-matched mate."

In a smaller voice, I confessed, "He forsook me, and then

the Alpha clique finished me off."

The shame of it burned through me. He might have been an asshole—even the moon goddess couldn't blind me to that—but he'd been my fated mate. That was supposed to matter above everything else.

Emotion flared in Cole's amber eyes, the yellow practically glowing. He kept his expression neutral, though, no hint as to what he was thinking.

"What a fucking idiot."

I laughed, startled. "I tell you my mate bullied me for years and rejected me, and that's your reaction?"

"He is *not* your mate." The ferocity of the words caught me off guard. I pulled back from Cole, wrinkling my brow at his sudden reaction. "He gave up the right by being a gods-damned moron."

That wasn't exactly how I'd put it, but it was nice to have someone say that. "You don't think it's pathetic? I was such a shit shifter he'd rather see me dead than be tied to me." I tried to make the words sound cavalier, but they fell flat. Mainly because, deep down, they were the truth of my thoughts.

"If he ever possesses a shred of wisdom, he'll regret that until the day he dies."

We sat in silence for a time. Without even realizing it, I'd shifted back to lean against Cole for support. He wasn't usually the touchy-feely type but clearly was making an exception for how distressed I'd been. Probably feeling guilty for dredging up these memories, though I'd never thought Cole to be *capable* of guilt.

"Do you want them all dead?" Cole asked casually, breaking the silence.

I blinked, startled from my own thoughts. "What?"

"If I were to kill them and drag their souls to Hell for your amusement. Would that please you?" He said it the same way he sometimes asked if I wanted the last brownie. Of course, half the time he'd see me eying it and snatch it up right after offering.

"This is just a hypothetical, right?" There was something deeply unnerving about how calmly he'd asked that.

"Naturally," he replied after a beat.

I was less than convinced but let it go. They were a realm away, and Cole was just an undead shifter like me.

Part of me wanted to say yes. I wanted to make them hurt. Make them feel the same pain they'd caused me. But it would never be the same. They'd been a pack while I'd been an outcast. There was a social element to every taunt, every jab that couldn't be replicated.

And truthfully, I didn't want to spend another minute thinking of them.

"They're not worth it. It won't change anything," I said at last. "Unless you think it would help me harmonize with my wolf. That was a joke," I quickly added, noting the glint in Cole's amber eyes.

"That could work," Cole mused. His arm had come to wrap around me. The heat of his body was almost soothing, a quiet reminder that he was here. *I* was here. Not trapped.

"It's just their nature," I insisted, trying not to sound bitter. "Alpha mixed with asshole says the weakling deserves what she gets." *I deserved it.*

"That is *not* an alpha's nature," Cole growled. "Alphas are there to lead. They're strong, not so they can put down the weak but to protect them."

The vehemence of his words forced me to truly consider them. Cole had a point. He was the most alpha-Alpha I'd ever met, and he could also be a giant asshole (see: taking the last brownie, coming up with the silver cage). Hell, he probably thought he was better than me, but he didn't shove it in my face. He'd rescued me from the nixie rather than let it pull me to Tartarus. He'd agreed to train me. Let me stay in his castle. And even if he kept several frustrating truths to himself, he'd at least given me some answers.

"And you're *not* weak," Cole said again.

A funny half-smile worked over my lips. "I know you feel bad for my freak-out when you're willing to flatter me."

"Do I seem like a male who wastes his breath on insincere words?"

"No," I conceded. *But you seem like a male with secrets.* I hadn't forgotten what I'd overheard. Maybe Cole was entitled to his privacy, but that didn't stop my need to seek out answers.

"Do you know how rare it is for a shifter to willingly face silver, little wolf?"

I poked his arm, which was wrapped over mine. "It's Avery."

I didn't have to see him to know his eyes were rolling. "My point is, few have the resolve to face it. You went willingly. Even if it was overwhelming, that was a powerful decision." A pause. "And for what it's worth, I'm sorry. I shouldn't have put you in that position, given your... background."

I let out a mock gasp that turned into a half-yawn. "An apology from his grumpiness himself? This might have all been worth it." He snorted, but there was an indulgent glint to his eyes. "I want to be strong, whatever it takes, even if I need to go back in that cage tomorrow." I shuddered slightly at the thought, even as resolve coursed through me.

Cole's grip tightened slightly. "I'll figure something else out." I made a sound of acknowledgment, leaning back. "You're exhausted." A statement laced with emotion I couldn't parse.

"Just need a nap," I muttered, slumping against Cole, my body sliding down slightly.

Cole made a noise halfway between a growl and cough. "The silver drained you. You should sleep."

I nodded absently. I felt like I'd run a marathon. Actually, that probably would've been easier given my shifter stamina.

My eyes fluttered shut against my will. I just wanted to curl up and sleep.

Cole shifted underneath me, inching away. I grabbed his arm. Call it exhaustion, or maybe I was simply feeling vulnerable after revealing my past to Cole. "Just... wait. Stay until I fall asleep."

Cole stopped moving away, though he adjusted slightly so his back was to the headboard and I was able to stretch out on top of the covers. He didn't speak. Halfway asleep, I asked Cole a question that had been circling in my mind since he'd told me what this realm was.

"How did you die?"

Maybe I should've asked something pointed, tried to understand the mysterious conversation I'd overheard. But for some reason, this mattered more.

Cole didn't answer for so long I thought he might ignore the question altogether. Wouldn't be the first time.

But then, just as I was at the fringes of unconsciousness, he spoke.

"I can't remember the last time I wasn't in Hell."

Chapter XXI

*T*HE FIELD WAS AT once familiar to me. I'd been there a few times, and it was always in my dreams.

I hadn't dreamed like this since my first days in Hell. Hadn't heard that subconscious voice that comforted—and often chastised—me.

I'd missed the voice. It's sad when one of your two friends is imaginary at the ripe age of twenty, but, well, one of mine was.

Normally, the voice spoke immediately as I started dreaming. But there was no sound on the field. The grass was taller than before, maybe eight inches. I wandered around barefoot, the blades tickling my ankles as I explored. No lake this time, or forest, but there were hills. It was odd not having someone to talk to.

I crested one hill and blinked.

Because there was a bed.

Random furniture wasn't entirely unexpected. Sometimes a table with food, sometimes a chair, though those things were rare.

But this wasn't any bed. No, I recognized the large,

four-poster frame. Bigger than a king-size. Rumpled sheets.

Cole's bed.

The first place I'd met him. Where he'd laid back with hooded, appraising eyes. The memory stirred something inside me. A want.

I took a step closer to the bed. It was a dream, after all. Who could say why my imagination conjured it up? I circled the bed, suspicious.

And then, from under the covers, "Come looking for me?"

The covers were suddenly gone, and there was Cole.

He wore nothing, a spare sheet just barely covered him. My imagination is really gonna censor this? I half-hissed at myself.

My blood seemed to flair as I drank in the sight. His cut muscles on display, even as he laid back, the picture of relaxation.

"This is just a dream," I said, more to myself than him.

"A dream," Dream-Cole echoed. "I suppose that'll do."

Then he sat up, the sheet falling away. And... fuck.

I had to wonder about Cole being a shifter because I wasn't sure we'd exactly fit. I slammed my gaze upwards. Oh my God. Why was I thinking about sex with Cole? The fact a dream version of him was currently naked in bed, looking utterly irresistible.

"There's no harm in looking your fill. You're hardly dressed like a nun," the male nearly purred. His voice was pure sex.

I looked down. I hadn't noticed what I was wearing, though I would've sworn it wasn't lingerie.

Yet now, two scraps of black lace were the only things covering me. And coverage was a generous term. A few strands of red hair that fell over my breasts offered more modesty than the nearly transparent balconette bra.

And Dream-Cole was looking. Blatant hunger shone in his amber eyes. On reflex, I crossed my arms over my chest. His lip quirked up at the gesture, spreading to a full grin as I put my arms back down since I felt silly.

Seriously, why was I covering myself? It was just a dream, and it's not like I had deep-rooted insecurities about my body. Not my human one, at least.

"I guess it's not that weird I'm dreaming of you," I said.

"Oh? You make a habit of it?" There was that flirtatious side that sometimes peaked out before Cole tamped down on it. My imagination was replicating it perfectly, if a bit less restrained.

"I was exhausted, and I'd been talking to you—the real Cole, I mean—before sleeping. It's not that weird." Never mind the fact I'd never dreamed of anyone else before. Until those dreams with the voice began, my periods of unconsciousness went without the punctuation of dreams. But maybe that was just a side effect of being in Hell.

"And you just happened to think of me naked in my bed."

I flushed, feeling silly. "It's just a piece of furniture. I was tired. That's probably why it's here."

The glint in his eye was familiar. It told me I'd just made some misstep. If we were sparring, Cole would be about to sweep my legs, knocking me down before I even realized what had happened. "Then there's no harm in joining me here. It is just a dream, as you said."

There was no mistaking the hunger in his eyes as he said that.

I didn't want to get into the bed with Cole. More accurately, I really, really wanted to hop into the bed and that was making me hesitant. But I wasn't one to back down once Cole had thrown the gauntlet.

I moved onto the bed. Cole, of course, didn't move so I could fit comfortably, so I wound up half on top of him as I sat down.

Well, it was just a dream. No reason for me to be uncomfortable. I moved closer, letting our limbs tangle as I leaned over him.

There weren't two ways about it. Cole was as glorious in my dreams as he was in real life. And here, I could admire—had been all but dared to. I stretched my fingers over his shoulder. Ran them over the beginning of the tattoo that wrapped around his body.

"I wonder what this is?" I mused. It was a design unlike any I'd seen before. More than simple lines, more like intertwined symbols. Too abstract to read.

My fingers trailed down the front of his chest. Cole lifted his other arm. At first, I thought he'd push my hand away, but instead, it came forward, under my chin, as he forced me to look away from the tattoo.

"Maybe I'll tell you for a kiss." There was that seductive

purr again, the one that sent a shiver down my spine, a shiver I couldn't hide from his consuming gaze.

"If only it were that easy to get answers from you."

"Try me." A dare.

Well, it was only a dream. In my dream, there was no point in pretending I didn't want to kiss Cole. No need to hide the way I wanted to run my hands through his hair or cover myself with his scent.

So without further hesitation, I rolled forward and captured the alpha's lips.

And fuck. What a kiss.

I'd never kissed someone before, but that didn't matter in a dream. In my dream, Cole guided me, urging me down. Nipping my lower lip. Suckling the pain into pleasure. Making me arch, making me want to claim his mouth the way he made his own mark on me. It left me breathless, in the dizzy way dreams do, where you're disoriented and wide-eyed and wondering how you got into this.

And goddess, if that was just a dream, what would reality be?

Cole wasn't content with a simple peck, and neither was I. I straddled him, my body instinctively moving to seat itself on top of him. His naked body under me was tantalizing. His cock pressed against me, the size... but of course I would imagine it that way. It might have been intimidating at first, but it felt so right. The thin scrap between my entrance and his erection was hardly a barrier, and I wondered just how far a dream could go.

Cole wasn't content to dominate my mouth, he wanted to feel my whole body. One hand gripped my hair, not so tight it was painful but with enough pressure that I arched against him. The other came to my front, fondling my breast through the bra, the friction of the fabric an erotic tease. My nipples were hard, begging for more. I reached one hand to soothe the ache, but Cole swatted it away with a growl. A clear message that I should keep my hands on him.

He broke the kiss, the sudden loss making me ache. He bent lower and took one swollen peak in his mouth, the bra suddenly gone. I bucked at the sudden contact, the sensation as delightful as it was foreign, but his grip held me in place. My moans were foreign sounds. I'd never felt this way, never knew it could be like this. He took his time with one side before switching.

"Fuck." I threw my head back, shutting my eyes as pleasure washed over me.

He pulled away after another moment. I ached for more, but something in Cole's eyes made me pause. It was more than animalistic lust. No, there was a depth, a knowing that made me still despite my body's need.

"You're the most beautiful creature I've ever seen." The words were quiet. Almost reverent.

He brushed a single lock of red hair that had fallen forward back behind my ear. The single movement was somehow more intimate than everything else, and I wasn't sure how to name the funny feeling in my chest and stomach.

But I didn't want to deal with that now. Now, if I was going to have a single, hot fantasy with Cole, I was going to take it for all it was worth.

I caught his lips in mine again, rocking forward over his erection, increasing the friction against my ache.

"I want you," I moaned against his lips. "Need to feel you."

He pulled aside and nipped my ear as if chastising me. "Not in a dream."

I growled, too worked up to tolerate denial. "It's my dream. I should get what I want."

"Then tell me what you want," he ordered me. For some reason, the command sent a bolt of need through me rather than the annoyance I normally felt when bossed around. Maybe just because I was worked up with desire.

You. I held back the answer, even to myself. "Pleasure."

I'd had so little of it in my life. Never at another's hands. Never even in a dream like this.

"Then pleasure you'll have." A vow.

Cole rolled us over, lifting himself on top of me. In a single movement, he'd pulled my hands up and held them in a vise. A move I'd been familiar with in sparring, but this was different.

This was... delicious.

His dominance seemed to fill the air. I breathed it in like it was salvation. He bent down to kiss me, I first thought, but instead, he only touched the edge of my mouth. Then another to the spot where my ear met my neck. My chin. My neck. Sucking, kissing, nipping. He laid a trail down my body, one that had me writhing in wanton desperation. I couldn't recognize the words coming from my mouth, the gasps, the moans. I was helpless against him, and I'd never enjoyed it more.

He went lower on my body, too low to hold my hands any longer, but somehow they were still pinned in place.

"Handcuffs?" I gasped as he pressed a kiss to my inner thigh.

"Making sure you behave." A hint of amusement in his words.

I bucked my hips, trying to center his kisses to where I needed them most. "Make me."

Cole paused his sweet torture only long enough to say, "I'll enjoy it."

Then he reached my center. And he licked it.

I went wild, wanting more contact, bucking my hips with need. His grip on my legs added to the pleasure as he held me against him, kissing, suckling, driving me mad. The scrap of fabric that had covered my mound had gone the way of the bra, disappearing into the ether. I didn't care. I just knew I needed him, needed the pleasure he'd promised to wring from me.

He praised my passion, offering sweet words in response. The dark-haired wolf enjoyed having me at his mercy.

"Good girl," he said as I groaned, nearly vibrating with pleasure.

"Make me come," I begged.

Cole paused, amber eyes capturing mine. "Ask nicely."

Even in his wildest dreams that wouldn't happen. "Now," was all I could growl.

He loosed a dark chuckle, then finally, he stopped teasing.

And I nearly combusted.

He pressed a kiss to my clit, more than a simple tease. No, he sucked and pulled, and then he sent me over the edge.

I saw stars.

And then it all disappeared.

Chapter XXII

I woke up with a start, panting. I scanned my empty bed wildly.

Empty being the key word.

It had just been a dream.

And what a dream it had been... *Tongues and claws and amber eyes that seared me.*

Mortification crashed through me. It's not that I was ashamed of my attraction to the Alpha male. Even if I was dead, I wasn't blind. But the intensity of that dream... I'd never experienced anything like that.

I inhaled, tasting his lingering scent on my tongue. No doubt the cause of my X-rated dream. That, and being emotionally frayed after the silver.

I made a dash for the bathroom as if he might show up any minute, even though he obviously hadn't been in the room for hours. Instinctively, I knew I'd slept for a long time, no doubt recovering from the aftereffects of my last disastrous training session.

I darted under the blast of water and scrubbed, washing

away any traces of my arousal. The last thing I needed was Cole scenting my thoughts. I'd never live it down. As it was, I'd been getting more than my fair share of teasing over the fact my wolf refused to do anything more violent than lick Cole.

As warm water sluiced over my body, I recalled the dream in flashes. It had been all too vivid. Cole's hands caressing me. My body responding. The touches had grown more intimate, the teasing more demanding. I'd woken up on the edge. I'd never felt passion like that. I had as healthy a sex drive as the next shifter, but I'd never really been the type to indulge it. There was no one to indulge it with, and though I *could* manage on my own, it had never been quite as tempting.

The warm water and memories lulled me. I rubbed a hand over my body, tempted to relive the fantasy.

But it was *Cole*.

The thought cut through the haze of lust that had settled over me. I practically rubbed my skin off with the remaining soap before jumping out of the shower. I climbed the stairs to the roof two at a time, proud of the way I now confidently navigated the castle.

You dreamed about him because you were exhausted, lonely, and his scent was some convenient inspiration for your subconscious, I told myself, bracing for seeing the wolf. *It doesn't mean anything.*

It had just been a dream. A filthy, wicked dream.

One I was going to absolutely bury in my mind while training with Cole today. Maybe he'd give me a break and have me do one of those solo tasks, like counting every book in the library while he stayed far away.

No luck. Cole was in training gear, already warming up on the bench press when I reached the roof.

He was magnificent in motion. There was something about the way he went about typical exercises that felt like a performance. Like he was always modeling them with his effortless, perfect form. That's all they were to him, after all, exercises. Not like when he fought and turned into an absolute beast.

I couldn't help but freeze for a moment as I stared. He was facing up, grinding out a few reps with a mind-numbing amount of plates on the bar, even for a shifter. The veins of his arms bulged with exertion, even as his chest moved in steady breaths. His shirt had ridden up with him laying back on the bench, exposing an expanse of skin with dark hair promising even more under his sweats.

I swallowed. I had dreamed about those exact promises.

"Did you come to train or to eye-fuck me?" Cole didn't even look at me as he called me on my ogling, instead, finishing out a final rep and racking the weight.

Caught. "I figured if you were going to show off, someone should appreciate it." I tried to sound snarky. Cool. Instead, my heart was already pounding in my chest. I tried for calming breaths, not wanting him to catch onto the accelerated beats and call me on them.

"That so?" He sat up, lifting his shirt to wipe his forehead. Not that he seemed to have broken a sweat. Was it a show for me? A taunt? A trap?

Because damn if it didn't work. My eyes latched onto the tight abs, the twisting tattoo. I could almost remember what it had been like to run my fingers over the raised figure.

That was just a dream. And it's not like he knew I fantasized about doing just that.

But Cole was definitely smirking when he finally pulled his shirt down.

Bastard.

He got up from the bench in one fluid motion, then gestured from me to the bench, a clear command.

When I didn't immediately move, he deigned to verbally order me. "Your turn."

I growled, not liking being ordered around. Especially when I was already on edge.

He didn't take the bait, just stared me down.

There was no sense arguing with him. I did want to train. So I walked over to the bench, refusing to break eye contact.

The corners of his lips twitched up as if amused by the internal battle waged inside me.

That smile. Those lips. Suddenly it was impossible to hold his gaze, so I turned my attention to the plates. Cole worked out with a truly impressive amount, so I removed about six plates before Cole stopped me with a hand on my wrist.

I flinched.

"Jumpy today," he remarked. I had to be imagining the knowing glint in his eyes, so I forced myself to relax. "This is good for today." He nodded to the weights on the bar.

I frowned. It was fifty pounds over my previous max.

"I might still be weak from the silver," I hedged.

"After all the hours you spent dreaming? I'm confident you've recovered."

The word choice was just a coincidence. I was seriously cursing that stupid dream. I laid down, expecting Cole to move back so I would have room to lift.

Instead, he came to stand directly behind my head. If I glanced back... well, I had quite the view. "But since you're worried, I'll spot you."

His scent was all around me. First, because I was laying in the spot he'd just been, but now he towered over me. My wolf side wanted to rub herself all over the space to get the scent on her. The human, the stupid human, wanted to inspect just what was behind my head.

I forced myself to keep looking straight up. "I'm good."

Cole peered over me, arms crossed as he looked down. "I insist." That cocky, teasing tone.

Why did he have to be in such a good mood this morning? If he were his usual asshole self, I'd be able to ignore the dream, a silver-induced hallucination, because that Cole would *never* have me in his bed, conjured up. This flirty version of Cole was all invitation. The Cole from yesterday, when he'd rescued me from the silver cage, had been caring, attentive.

And my defenses were weak to that.

Needing a distraction, I gripped the bar and started to lift. To my surprise, I was able to manage the weight he'd left for me.

Cole murmured his approval. "Good girl."

"Good girl," he'd said as I'd moaned, body consumed by pleasure.

My grip faltered. Cole snatched the bar away before it could hurt me.

"Focus," he chastised.

As if I could! Not with his scent all around me. But I forced out a few reps anyway, rushing through them faster than he'd normally approve of. After my third set of a dozen, I shoved the bar up for him to rack and sat up, edging to the other side of the bench.

"I want to do something other than lifting weights," I declared.

Cole's gaze narrowed. That wasn't how our dynamic worked. He ordered, and I obeyed because, as he liked to remind me, he was older, stronger, and the more experienced shifter. But whatever. Let him yell at me. I couldn't take it anymore.

But Cole didn't call me out on it. "Fine." He moved from his place behind the bench and came to my side, once again towering over me. I was forced to crane my neck.

"Shift."

I blanched.

"Shift," he repeated.

I practically jumped off the bench for some more distance. "That won't do me any good."

Cole cocked a brow. "Really? The little wolf who needs to become a stronger shifter doesn't think shifting is a good use of her time?"

"I do shift," I argued. In my room. Being in the small space wasn't ideal, but my wolf couldn't be trusted around Cole. Hell, I barely could today and I wasn't feeling the least bit wolfy.

"An enclosed space doesn't do shit for honing your skills," Cole countered.

How did he know? Then again, it's not like I was leaving the castle.

"The roof is still kind of enclosed." The argument was weak to my own ears.

"Then we'll put you in the woods later," Cole said, to my surprise. "But I want you to shift now."

"I can't."

"Can't? Or won't?" Cole wasn't the type to give even an inch.

"It's embarrassing," I ground out.

"What? That when you shift you want to hump me?"

I didn't need a mirror to know my cheeks had just turned beet red. I only hoped the hazy red sky was covering the blush. "That's my wolf, not me."

"And, little wolf, I keep telling you—you're one and the same."

Given the way I was panting after Cole as a human, that was becoming painfully clear. One wet dream and I wasn't able to think straight. Pathetic.

"I'll do it in the woods like you said. It'll be more normal." It had to be. This castle, with its creepy statues and ornery Alpha was enough to drive any shifter crazy. If I was able to run in the fresh air—weird to say about Hell—like I had when I'd first come, no doubt I'd feel normal. "We can even go now." Anything to get off this roof.

"Tomorrow. But you're going to have to do something to make up for disobeying me today, twice, with the weights and now shifting."

My mind went all kinds of places when he said that.

It did not, as it so happened, go to an urn full of soapy water, a gray sponge, and the foyer of the castle.

"Do I look like Cinderella to you?" I demanded as he led me there. "And isn't this whole castle magically self-cleaning?"

There was no warning. One second, I was mouthing off,

the next Cole had me pinned to a wall. His face was inches from mine, the slight stubble around his chin close enough to touch. He wedged himself between my hips, holding me up while one hand pressed against my throat. Not choking, but with a clear threat.

"If you want me to keep training you, you won't go against me a third time today." He bared his teeth, snapping them inches from my neck. Like he was thinking about biting it.

My breaths grew shallow.

"And despite what you may say, you do want me to train you. And I don't particularly relish in having your soul fall to Tartarus because you can't defend yourself." He paused, hand loosening. "Now, are you going to do as you're told?"

I ground my teeth before I could muster up a response other than let me fucking go. That would not produce the desired outcome.

"Yes," I hissed. *This* time, I'd do it. No promises in the future.

Cole let me go with surprising gentleness. I went over to the basin that had magically appeared and wet the sponge inside it.

***

"Not that I'm going against you, or whatever has shoved the stick up your butt, but what's the point of this?" I gestured to the segment of the cleaned floor I'd spent fifteen minutes working on. Weight training, endurance exercises, sparring, even the statues I understood. This?

"It's to motivate you to shift the next time I tell you to," Cole said easily from his perch against the wall where he absently flipped through some book.

Asshole.

Scrubbing the floor was tedious, boring, and made my wrists ache, but I'd be damned before I whined about it to Cole. There was no way to tell the time in the firelit room, but given how slow I was—and how quick Cole was to critique any so-called sloppiness—it took me ages to finish.

I made a grand gesture to Cole when I finished, presenting the useless fruits of my labor with a flourish. His lips tugged up as if to laugh before he schooled his features back to neutrality and gave me a cool nod.

Whatever. "Now that you're done torturing me, I'm going to get some dinner." Just the thought made my stomach rumble, and I turned away from that returning lip quirk thing Cole had going on today. Maybe he had a tick. In any case, I hadn't eaten in hours.

Cole, to my surprise, didn't immediately vanish after my training was done the way he normally did. He pushed off the wall and followed me down the hall to the kitchen. "I'll remind you, torture is done in the basement, not up here."

Hilarious. A guy lives in Hell and torture jokes are supposed to be funny. Actually, he'd made a similar joke before. "Is your basement actually a dungeon?" I asked, curious.

What would be the point?

Cole didn't deny it.

"Oh my goddess, it totally is."

I opened the door to the magical kitchen and beelined for one of the perfectly cooked steaks set on the table.

"It's a normal feature in a castle," he said mildly.

The steak was good. I groaned, swallowing a bite. Cole's ever-watching amber eyes clocked the movement and for some reason, I felt myself blushing.

I tried to take the next bites more discreetly, which was hard since the bastard had starved me all day.

"I want to check it out," I said between bites. Why shouldn't I check it out? I was here for the time being.

"Absolutely not." The tone brooked no argument.

So naturally, I argued. "Why not? What's down there?"

"No one and nothing you need to worry about."

My jaw dropped open. "Hold on, you're telling me you have people in your dungeon?"

"Avery, I'm serious. Don't go down there." He was dodging all my questions, which was an answer in itself.

"Don't concern yourself with it."

Anger rose inside me, a fast flash that made me curl my hands into fists. I loathed having secrets kept from me. "Like I don't need to concern myself with demons?"

"Exactly," Cole growled. "Unless you're delusional enough to beat me sparring."

"I'm never going to be able to do that," I snarled back. "It doesn't make me weak. It just makes you freakishly strong."

Cole said nothing. Didn't act cocky when I'd called him strong, didn't push it.

Conversation over. Our plates were empty, and for once I didn't feel like grabbing seconds. I pushed myself away from the chair, gazing out the nearby window. The red sky had set to the nighttime hues.

"I don't want to be weak," I murmured to myself. I was sick of it, but no matter how much I trained, it didn't feel like I was making any progress.

Cole got up, shoving his chair back as he stood. For a moment I felt his gaze, then he started to leave.

I'd have missed his words, thought I'd imagined them if he hadn't paused at the doorway for just a moment to look back at me.

"I'll make you strong." A quiet vow.

And then he was gone. And I was alone again.

I sank back in the chair. In one moment, he was caring, tender, or teasing. But the next I'd want to go ten rounds with him, even if it meant I'd wind up on my ass. Everything in me was in chaos. My emotions. My body.

But in my mind, there was only one way forward. Cole had told me not to go somewhere. Forbidden it.

So that settled it.

The next chance I had, I'd be headed to the basement.

Chapter XXIII

COLE PUSHED ME PARTICULARLY hard the next few days. It was impossible to track the time in any precise measurements in Hell—days, weeks. They ran together into a repetitive tangle. I didn't forget about my goal to explore forbidden corners of the castle, but it was like he was keeping me too tired to get into trouble.

There was no doubt I was getting stronger, but at the same time, there was almost a block. Sometimes I was so in tune with my wolf side. I got better at sharpening my senses. My reflexes were faster. If I came across any of my old packmates, I could probably hold my own, even if Cole continued to effortlessly pin me when we sparred.

But those times when I should've been fighting with everything I had, wolf and human combined, it was like there was a block.

Cole had noticed as well, and he increasingly voiced his criticisms. Finally, one day he made good on his threat to send me to the woods to shift.

We'd had a relatively easy morning session, which I

should've taken as a warning. The red haze set and gave way to night as Cole led me back to those front gates.

I hadn't stepped foot outside, not since the nixie. Cole had made it clear he would not be happy if I disobeyed him, and for once, I'd been willing to not push him on it.

This evening, we'd both stayed in our sweats. The dark gray pants hung low, revealing another flash of tattoo. I forced myself to stay focused on the door. I'd stuck with clothing I wouldn't mind having torn to shreds.

"Be back in three hours," Cole said, opening the door.

I stared at him in disbelief. "That's it?" Okay, he'd already explained the basic exercise this morning—go into the woods and practice shifting back and forth. Let my wolf run without allowing those instincts to entirely overrun *me*. I'd kind of expected more. "Where will you be? Back here?"

"Going to miss me, little wolf?"

I turned to look over the drawbridge, breathing in a steadying breath. No way was I going to let him read into my nerves. "You do have a habit of reminding me that if anything in the woods so much as blinks at me, I'm going to turn into a pile of intestines."

"You're not quite that weak," Mr. Supportive offered.

I rolled my eyes.

"I'll be around." With that, Cole turned away from the door.

And I was left to face the outside on my own.

Good. This was a *good* thing, I tried to convince myself. I couldn't let myself get in the habit of relying on Cole.

And this would be my reminder.

I took hesitant steps across the drawbridge, feeling the heat of the lava moat as I exited.

With my enhanced senses, I tasted the scents in the air. For being, well, Hell, it was actually kind of pleasant. Nothing alarming. I jogged in the direction of the woods. Already, my wolf was close to the surface. I held her back, not wanting to give in to the shift until I decided.

The woods were maybe a mile away. Once inside, it was time to shift. I felt oddly hesitant. When I'd first arrived in Hell, I'd been in my wolf form. It had been the single most liberating experience I'd ever had. I'd finally felt like the shifter I was meant to be. Except I had no control over the shape. I'd tried to force control in my bedroom, shifting each morning, but my wolf didn't enjoy the confinement. There was no telling what would happen once I gave her free rein.

I shucked my clothing off and left it in a pile.

Here goes nothing. The shift wasn't as effortless as I remembered it being at first, but sure enough, a moment later I was a wolf. I glanced down at my red-fur paws, the most visual reminder of my outcast status in Moon-Ghost.

As a wolf, I explored the forest. Cole hadn't exactly provided an overabundance of instructions except that I should shift back and forth to build stamina.

My wolf had other plans. There was the scent of rabbit, low to the ground. I stalked forward, utterly patient as I spied my prey.

One powerful leap later and Thumper was no more.

On the bright side, he tasted delicious.

Curious how I'd feel shifting after a meal, I returned to my human form. The pride that I'd felt as a wolf ebbed slightly, but besides that, I felt normal.

I explored the forest on foot for a while longer, not minding the fact I was nude. There were no other signs of life in the forest, which was fine by me.

Another hour passed with me shifting once again back and forth between forms. The rapid shifts were slightly exhausting, but with each one, I felt more in control. It was easier to retain my rational brain in wolf form, and tapping into my wolf sense in human form was effortless.

I scanned the empty forest. A new scent had come over on the air.

One I didn't recognize.

It was almost feline, but given that I hadn't come across many cats living in a pack of wolf shifters, I couldn't be sure.

A part of me was half tempted to call out to Cole in hopes he was "around." But ego stopped me, even before the common sense against yelling with a potential threat nearby. No, I didn't need Cole to save me. Least of all when I wasn't even sure what I'd need saving from.

It could just be a house cat, right? There were rabbits after all. Why not other small mammals?

I stayed in my human form, trying to isolate the scent. It grew thicker from all sides. Fuck. Was I being circled?

I scanned the dark woods, but there were no signs to detect.

Then, a rustle, close enough for me to identify.

It came from above.

I looked up and froze. Up in the trees was a creature with a lion's mane and structure, but the face was nearly human. Disfigured.

And once I spotted it, the creature hopped down from the tree and landed fifteen feet in front of me.

There was no mistaking its intent. Aggression rolled off the creature in waves.

The lion let loose a massive roar, loud enough to make the tree branches shake. Its orange eyes glowed with a killing urge. I had a single second to make a decision—run or fight.

And I'd decided long ago not to run again.

I squared my shoulders, not willing to wait for the lion creature to make the first move. I launched myself forward.

By the time I landed on the lion with a snarl, I was a wolf.

Instinct took over as I landed on the lion. I dug my claws into the back of the lion, who arched itself to throw me off. I beat it to the punch, jumping off with a growl.

There was no time for questions. What the creature was,

why it had been stalking me. No, there was only the battle.

The lion creature was twice my size, but I was faster. It charged at me and I dodged left. Adrenaline pumped through me. I felt utterly in sync with my wolf, able to trust those instincts and refine them with my weeks of training. I might not have trained in wolf form, but the principles were the same: hit hard and don't let yourself get caught.

I lunged for the lion before it could recover from the charge.

I couldn't grip the neck. Instead, I targeted its heels, which were less protected by the thick coat. If I could weaken those powerful haunches, I could hobble it. I circled the creature, darting in and out to nip at the heels until blood poured freely. The lion roared in anger. I matched it with a snarl.

The lion spun with unexpected agility on my next dart in, catching me off guard. I fell backward, narrowly dodging the massive teeth that wanted to rip into my jugular.

Fuck. This wasn't cutting it.

I couldn't afford to use up my stamina, winning with little nips. Aside from the unexpected lunge, the lion was moving more slowly. But at this rate, it would take hours to bleed the creature dry. I didn't have that kind of time.

No, I needed a way to win. But how? I couldn't penetrate the thick mane.

The lion roared, preparing to charge. Suddenly, a plan occurred to me. It was a long shot. I backed up, acting like I was exhausted. The lion took the bait. It charged me.

I forced myself to stay exactly where I was.

Twenty feet.

Fifteen feet.

Ten feet away, the lion sprang forward, moving from a run to a leap.

Now that the lion had committed, I crouched and surged forward.

The lion slammed into the tree that had been behind me. It gave me all of a two-second reprieve. I'd maneuvered under the lion's belly when it landed, and I turned onto my back. With one vicious slash, I clawed the underbelly. I tore into the exposed flesh with my teeth. The lion sank. I barely made it out from under before the body managed to pin me.

I shook myself off and inspected the lion. Its orange eyes were sightless, the scent of aggression replaced by blood and death.

Holy cheeseballs.

I'd just taken down this lion creature.

I shifted back, my human body slick with sweat. I wanted to get a view and my wolf lacked the ability to scan as effectively.

"Nicely done. A bit sloppy, but decent enough."

I spun at the sound of the voice.

Cole.

He leaned back against a tree only a few feet away, still in sweats. He ran a hand through those dark, messy curls like his biggest issue was a stray hair falling into his eye. He almost looked... pleased.

"What the fuck? You were lurking around but wouldn't give me a hand?" I demanded.

"You had it handled."

Any other time, the vague compliment might've filled me with pride. But this had been a fight to the death. "This wasn't a training exercise! I was attacked, asshole."

The male said nothing, and I read the meaning of the silence.

"Wait, was this a training exercise? You set me up?"

"I didn't set you up," Cole said, annoyance clear in his tone. "But yes, I arranged for the Leo demon to approach you."

I stopped listening. Fury turned the woods red, and I threw myself at Cole.

I didn't shift, not the way I had with the lion, but I was all wolf. And for once, my wolf side was as angry as I was with Cole. I snarled, gripping his shirt with my fists. "You bastard, you tried to kill me!"

The anger in Cole's eyes matched my own, the only warning I had before he threw me back against another tree, reversing the pin.

"I showed you what you're capable of," Cole countered with a snarl. "You needed to see what it's like to stop overthinking and be in sync with both sides."

"Capable?" I hissed. "I'll show you just how capable I am."

With power I didn't know I possessed, I tossed Cole off. Green sparks flew in his wake, but I ignored them, lunging to where he'd landed against the tree. I got right up close. I shoved my palms into his shoulders. God, this male. No one had ever infuriated me the way he did.

Cole, for his part, didn't look angry at the way I'd tossed him across the small clearing. No, he actually looked... pleased.

"Can't argue with results," was his simple reply.

"I damn well can. You set a demon on me!"

"And you handled it just as I knew you would. If you'd been in any actual danger, I'd have stepped in." There was a calming confidence to his words that should have been a balm. A promise that he had my back.

But could I really take his words at face value? "I don't think I've ever been this angry." The wolf in me was still baring her teeth. I didn't like being set up. If he'd wanted to orchestrate this showdown, fine, but could he have at least given me a heads-up? Why keep this information to himself?

"Guess what, little wolf? I don't care if you're angry with me. Not if it means you're strong enough to defend yourself," Cole finished with a growl.

"I don't think I've ever met anyone as vexing as you," I bit out.

"The feeling's entirely mutual."

And then I couldn't say which of us moved first, but suddenly our mouths collided.

Chapter XXIV

H E TASTED LIKE DOMINANCE. Like lust, anger, and victory all rolled into one.

An utterly intoxicating combination, one I drank in with desperation. The kiss was an entirely different battle, one where I was unsure of my footing but unwilling to give up. I wanted to taste. To touch. To be swallowed whole.

Cole moved us so fast I could barely process the movement, spinning me around so my back was to the tree. One strong hand pinned my wrists above my head. A position that was almost familiar, even though there was no reason it should've been. I didn't feel the wood digging into my naked back, only arched to feel him against me, to have as little space between us as possible. Cole wedged himself between my hips which opened in need.

I was powerless to pull my hands away, to run my claws down his back the way I craved, so instead, I did all I could with my tongue to convey my feelings.

Desire.

Want.

Need.

I'd never felt like this. Never been so blinded by my urges. If I thought I'd been hot from one wet dream, the real thing turned my core molten. Cole's free hand came to my breast, squeezing, teasing the peak that was hard from arousal.

"Fuck," Cole breathed against my lips. "You taste incredible."

"Less talking," I demanded, recapturing his lips. I could feel them curve against me into a smirk.

I nipped his lips in reprimand. The taste of his blood in my mouth did nothing to cool my desire. If anything, it simply whets it.

It spurred Cole on, the kiss turning rougher. My lips would be bruised, no doubt. But I wanted more. More sensation. More touching. More Cole.

It was a violent thing, the kiss. Frustration had been brewing between us for weeks, and rather than a gradual release, this was an explosion. I moaned against his mouth, gasping as Cole flicked his tongue in a way that could've sent me to Hell all over again. I writhed against him, unable to help myself.

If I'd been a cat shifter, I might've purred.

But I was a wolf, and with this alpha, I submitted. I let him take, let him demand. Not without resistance, but ultimately, I succumbed and let him take the lead. His physical power was overwhelming me, pleasing me in a way I hadn't known I'd craved. He was suddenly everything, an endless ocean of scent and touch and sensation, and I wanted to drown in him.

It felt so right. So damn *right*.

I pulled back. The thought was like cold water over my head.

"Something wrong?" Cole's eyes were hooded, orbs of pure seduction.

I tore my gaze away. "This is just a physical thing, right? Letting off steam?"

Because it couldn't be more. I couldn't have more with Cole. Kissing, even sex, would be fine. But I was in Hell, he'd just set a demon on me, and more than that, Cole was keeping secrets.

"Letting off steam," Cole echoed, relaxing his grip on my wrists slightly.

I nodded, desperate to recapture my breath. For some reason, I couldn't breathe. Could barely look at the male in front of me. "Right." Words had never felt so wrong, but I'd be a bigger fool than I'd ever been in Moon-Ghost to let myself believe this could be more. "Because we don't like each other like that. I drive you crazy. You're an asshole half the time. This is just... lust or whatever." A foreign sensation up until I'd laid eyes on Cole.

Cole drew back, releasing my wrists in a sudden jerk. He didn't pull his hand back entirely but rather kept it raised in the space between us, inches from my face. A part of me wanted to lean into the touch. A large, desperate, hungry part that had been caged for twenty years. A part that thought I could belong.

"Just lust," Cole agreed.

Something flashed over his face as he said the words, something that in any other circumstances, I'd have called sorrow. Regret, maybe.

I nodded, wishing I was happier we'd settled in. I mean, even lust was pretty awesome if that kiss was anything to go by. I mean, holy shit, talk about a first kiss. Deep in my bones, I knew no other kiss could compare. Might as well enjoy it with Cole while it lasted.

But the moment was gone. Cole didn't lean in to kiss me again.

I shivered, suddenly cold and exposed in a way I hadn't felt a moment ago.

I F I THOUGHT THINGS were going to improve after that, I was sorely mistaken.

On the one hand, Cole's plan had worked. I felt more in sync with my wolf side. Having found a critical balance fighting the Leo demon, I was able to balance both sides with more ease. We still disagreed on Cole, of course. My wolf wanted to turn and nuzzle him every chance she got. The human was less sure.

There'd been no further discussion about the kiss, which suited me fine. Or it would if I could stop thinking about it.

Seriously, how was I supposed to move on from a kiss like that? It was like I'd been lit on fire and all that was left of me was smoke. Swallowed. Demolished. It wasn't an altogether pleasant feeling, especially when I had to live with the knowledge it was a one-time deal.

Cole, for his part, was especially ornery in the days that followed. His words were short, his looks measured to keep me at length. Despite having exposed me to an actual demon, he refused to discuss any further until I pinned him. Even if I'd managed to beat the Leo demon, we both knew that wasn't happening any time soon.

A silly, naive part of me thought the kiss could've meant something to him. Nothing romantic, but maybe affection? Enough that he might open up and share the wealth of knowledge he kept locked away.

But there was no affection, only ice and granite. It had been an angry kiss. That's what I kept reminding myself.

Yet when I replayed that night in the forest over and over again in my head, anger was the furthest feeling from what I felt.

Now?

I just felt lost.

Another morning's training session had come and gone, complete with Cole's new foul mood. I'd hit a breaking point.

I was improving, dammit, but he refused to so much as acknowledge it. At one point, I'd overestimated my newly honed strength, and the barbell had slipped from my grip. Cole had snatched it away and thrown it halfway across the roof.

The four-hundred-pound bell had left a sizable crater in the roof.

I'd opened my mouth to thank Cole, and instead, the male had the nerve to snap his teeth and growl at me to watch it. I'd snarled back. The words, I didn't remember them. Just the fact it was becoming clear we were farther apart than before. And before, we'd barely been a step above acquaintances.

Which meant it was time to move on with my plan. If Cole wasn't going to give me answers, I was going to find them for myself.

The library had been my first source, but there was too much. I read through subject after subject. Poisonous plants and gemology and portals and demons, but for all that I read, I was no closer to finding actionable information.

Which meant it was time to look elsewhere.

And I knew the perfect place to start.

Cole had warned me off the basement-slash-dungeon more than once. It was hard to imagine he actually kept anyone down there. I mean, surely I'd have heard something. But with the magic of the castle, maybe not.

My inborn curiosity demanded answers, in any case. I

waited until nightfall. I made a point to hang out in the library for several hours, then headed to my room. Nothing out of the ordinary.

Then I rose from my bed and began to retrace my steps to the entrance of the basement. My scent map of the statues led me to a terrifying-looking creature at a faraway staircase. The creature had wings like a bat, with six-inch talons and massive claws. The face was too disfigured for me to make sense of whether it was male or female, but the scent under the stone simply said *danger*.

Fitting, because something told me if Cole found me sneaking into his dungeon, he'd be pissed.

So I won't let him catch me, I resolved.

The castle wasn't the brightest, cheeriest place, in general. The windows let in the red haze of hell, and the hanging sconces lit the hallways without ever seeming to need to be lit. Not exactly warm and welcoming, but it was fine. Even had a charm I'd gotten used to in my time here.

The stairs to the basement made the rest of the castle look like a sun-filled temple.

There was just enough light for my enhanced shifter eyes to make out the walls and steps and not stumble to my death. The air smelled different, stale and damp. How had I not noticed before? But then again, I'd stayed away at Cole's order.

The stairs continued for longer than one flight. Longer than ten. It took several minutes to reach the base, especially as I moved on light, silent footsteps. When I finally reached the base, I was in the middle of a hallway. The wall right in front of the stairs wasn't smooth stone like the rest of the castle. I took a step closer, drawing out my enhanced shifter vision in the night.

Thousands of little stones were embedded in the wall. A mural. And not a simple decorative one. This was one with a story, though I wasn't sure what it meant. The left depicted a forest of dead trees. On the right, a vibrant contrast of trees and plants, all in bloom. The center had two wolves sitting, facing each other.

A black one, the darkest color of night, with yellow stones for eyes.

And a red one.

I'd never heard of another red wolf. And I'd only ever met one wolf with fur as dark as night with amber eyes.

My enhanced hearing picked up the hiss of water coming from my right. That was as good a place to start searching, anyway. I was relieved to get away from the mural. The mural was a puzzle. Already I had more questions than answers, the opposite of what I needed. Especially while I was sneaking around the castle in the middle of the night.

The hallways underneath the castle were narrower than above. Darker. An invisible awareness crawled over my skin, making me want to turn back. Still, I forced myself in the direction of the sound of water.

"Is someone there?" a faint, frightened voice called. "Please! Answer me!"

Holy shit. Cole *was* keeping prisoners down here.

Emotions stabbed at me through the shock of the realization. Betrayal was the most potent.

How could he? For all his talk about alphas taking care of the weak, he was like the rest. It was already Hell, for moon's sake. Why lock them away down here?

"I'm coming!" I said, taking off after the voice. The sound of water disappeared, but the voice had come from the same direction. They'd sounded so scared.

After I turned the next corner, I reached the dungeon.

There was no denying it. Solid iron bars lined the hall on both sides, stretching back endlessly.

"Help me," the voice called again. Female. I lifted my foot to take a step closer, then hesitated.

Of course, in my initial shock, I'd failed to consider there might be a reason Cole kept them down here. They could be dangerous. But again, what in Hell wasn't? Cole had orchestrated the Leo demon's demise through me. Maybe he was colder, more callous than I'd ever realized. Maybe he'd identified whatever was in this dungeon as a threat and left it to rot. It was inhumane.

I could almost hear his voice. *Inhumane? Welcome to Hell, little wolf.*

"Please," the female begged. "Just come closer. Look at me.

Take pity on me, it's been so long since I've seen another creature."

Anguish lashed through me. I'd known that feeling. To be so alone.

It wasn't like I was going to let whatever creature out. But I'd gone down here to find answers. I'd just get close enough to see her but far enough away that she couldn't attack me through the bars. I mean, she sounded too pitiful to do even that, but so had the nixie.

"Okay, I'm coming," I said. "No funny business. Who are you?"

I walked carefully down the hallway. The figure was in the last cell on the left. I could just make out the outline at a distance. She didn't face me, not right away.

"Who am I?" the creature repeated.

"I'm Avery," I said, figuring there was no harm in introducing myself. "And I'm wondering what your name is."

I stopped in front of her cell, a good three feet from the bars. The rest of the cell block was silent. I didn't scent any blood or decay. No illness festered in these halls. No, they were clean, and the female smelled healthy.

But there was something off about her. Something almost reptilian.

The sound of water got louder, the hiss of it growing.

And then the creature turned around. And I realized it wasn't water I was hearing at all.

No, that was the sound of a hundred snakes spouting from the female's head, hissing at me.

"It's been so long since anyone had to ask." She sashayed closer. Her dress was a long piece of cloth, cinched at the shoulders and draped around luscious curves. I met her gaze, and there was such raw joy in her expression I almost took a step back.

Almost. Except I suddenly couldn't move my feet.

"I'm known as Medusa. Maybe you've heard of me?"

I tried to glance down at myself. It was impossible to physically move my head. You don't realize how natural that little movement when you glance down is until you're immobilized.

My body still looked normal, but I couldn't move an inch. Only my eyes could shift around. I flicked them back to the snake-haired creature. *What the fuck?* I wanted to scream. But I couldn't even move the vocal cords required to do that. A slight croak passed my lips. The most I could muster.

She leaned one shoulder against the bar, running a finger up and down the length of the iron bar. "Petrification, dear. It's a bit of a slow process in your case, but in a few moments, you'll turn to stone completely."

Oh goddess, the *statues*. The creepy statues in every shape that were scattered across the castle. That was why they smelled. They'd once been alive, like me.

"Nothing personal," she said absently. "But I've been here a very long time. Something about indiscriminate petrification being frowned upon by his majesty. Not that I can help it. Sunglasses look awful with my bone structure. I'm due a little vengeance, don't you agree?"

I risked another glance at my body. The tips of my nails were darkening into granite.

Shit. Shit, shit, shit. "It's not so bad. Well, it is. But there's nothing to be done now, so just settle and let it happen. Stop fighting it." She chastised me like she was lecturing a pup.

I tried to gasp for breath. I was choking, my lungs frozen in my body without the ability to cough. I was going to die here. Or worse, not die, live the rest of my days encased in stone.

I mustered all of my strength, drawing on my last mental reserves, and forced out one single breath, one word.

"Cole."

Medusa's eyes widened in shock, her snakes looking at each other and then back at me as if equally stunned. It would've been funny if I wasn't turning to stone. I couldn't feel my legs anymore.

There was nothing for a moment. Silence. Quiet.

This is the end for me.

The castle shook. An earthquake in Hell? I couldn't move, couldn't take shelter. The shaking grew more violent. The iron groaned as stone pressed down. Dear moon goddess, was this dungeon going to collapse?

And then Cole arrived.

I wasn't sure how I knew, but I sensed him a second before he came into view. I couldn't breathe in his scent with my stiff body, couldn't turn to see him.

But he was there. And something in my soon-to-be stone body unclenched.

"Avery!" There was an unrecognizable note in his voice. Something like panic.

He gripped my bicep. The muscle didn't give.

I could only see him from the corner of my eye. His face contorted into a terrible expression. He loosed a snarl, more fearsome and angrier than any he'd ever directed at me.

"How dare you!"

Medusa cackled. "I was due for some vengeance. You left me locked up for centuries. Imagine my good fortune—"

But she never finished gloating. One second she was there, the next the walls were painted in golden blood.

I wanted to speak, wanted to plead with Cole. To end me properly and put me out of my misery. To hold me as the stone overtook me.

"You're going to be okay," Cole growled.

If I could've moved, I'd have rolled my eyes and told him secrets were bad enough, but to move onto bald-faced lies?

But I couldn't move.

And a second later, I stopped perceiving altogether.

CHAPTER XXV

M Y EYES WERE OPEN, but I couldn't see through them clearly. Everything was a haze, fading in and out of darkness.

My leaden body was lifted. Cole? Was he going to use me to replace his barbell when I finished turning into a statue?

Curse after curse left his mouth as he moved me. The words spilled over me, my only tether to consciousness.

"Dammit, Avery, stay with me," he growled.

Telling me what to do? Good luck with that. I couldn't voice my thoughts to him, though, even as they surged to answer his demands. *Why do you even care?*

Cole didn't answer my silent question. He took me farther. Up the stairs, out of the castle. Miles crossed in minutes. I felt the distance more like a wind in my hair than anything else.

I missed most of the journey. My thoughts were sluggish. It reminded me of the one time Daphne and I had gotten drunk on the pack's moonshine, stolen from her parent's reserve. We'd laughed for hours until we puked up on the roof, spilling our guts into her mother's carefully tended garden.

This was way less fun.

We reached some barrier. A wall? Doors, maybe? If so, they were massive. I couldn't lift my gaze to see the top. Cole let out a roar that seemed to shake the ground. Wordless? Or was he saying a word? It was hard to understand.

Everything was sluggish. I just wanted to rest.

The doors opened as if on command, and Cole brought me through.

Another castle?

Maybe that was just the *thing* to have in Hell. A castle and the urge to kill me.

Cole strode through the hall, the heavy pound of his steps slamming through my dim conscious.

"Save her," he demanded. I'd never heard him sound like that. It wasn't just an alpha's command. It was stronger. It didn't just urge obedience, it assumed it.

I couldn't see anything. My vision kept going white, and this time it stayed for longer than any time before. Was this my new reality? Would I take up residence in some other dark corner of the castle?

The answer to Cole's demand came in the form of a lilting, feminine voice.

"How quick you are to order me."

In the back-most corner of my mind, an almost extinguished conscious part, I thought she sounded familiar.

"Help me, witch."

The woman *tsked*. "That's not my name. I don't forsake mine as easily as you do."

"*Hecate.*" The word was barely human. It promised the same violence that had painted the cell with Medusa's blood.

I forced myself to look with my glazed eyes. Just a flash of a figure appeared before they frosted over. A woman, a stunning beauty, in a purple gown that clung to every full-figured curve.

Then it was gone. I felt cold. So cold.

Empty.

"You haven't even asked my price."

"I don't care what it costs, just save her, godsdamn you." The desperation in his voice was startling, even as the conversation was so far away.

"It's not every day you see your king beg like this." Another click of her tongue. "I'll heal her. If you both stay for dinner. That's my price."

A loud growl. "Whatever. Just *do it* already."

My body moved. I thought my senses had almost entirely receded, but I still noted the distance from Cole.

"Shoo," the witch—Hecate—said.

"I'm not leaving her side."

"Well, I'm not healing while you pace like a lunatic. Give me peace and she will be well. You have my word."

Another growl. Cole was gone.

And I faded all the way down.

I WAS DROWNING IN all-consuming darkness. No light, no noise, no sensation. I had no skin, no sight.

Was I dreaming, or was this simply my new reality?

Strangely, I wasn't panicking. Instead, I was content to let it consume me. There was nothing to rebel against, so why bother? I could keep sinking here, away from the world, forever. The thought should've been terrifying, but all that was left was numbness.

"Stay with me, little wolf," a voice said. The first sound I'd ever heard.

Finally, something I could focus on. The familiar voice of my subconscious. As ever, it made me feel less lonely. Just like when I'd been passed out in the lockers or sleeping lightly in my bed at home, the voice found me and made me less alone.

Maybe if this was my new eternity, tortured by this darkness while my body had turned to stone, it wouldn't be so bad. Not if I had the voice with me.

"Don't even think that," the voice demanded.

I would've smiled, but I wasn't sure I had a body. "Always so bossy. What does it matter?"

The voice's reply was deathly serious. "You swore you'd never give in again. Never run from your problems. Are you going to start now?"

The words lit a fire in me. Not the solid blaze I was used to, but an ember. Better than nothing.

"I don't respond well to being bossed around."

"No, you never have, but believe me when I say it's in your best interest to stay here. If you let your mind drift off, I may not be able to get you back."

Get me back? The gentle urging confused me. "Is it drifting now?"

"I've anchored you for now," the voice explained. "But you need to come back on your own power. I can't pull you myself."

"How?" I asked. There was nothing here. Just bleak darkness that stifled all my senses.

"Find me. Follow my voice and wake up."

"You'll be with me?" I wasn't sure why I asked. I wasn't even sure what was being asked of me.

"I'll be with you," the voice promised.

The words steadied me in the endless, sinking sea. I held onto them, the tone, the promise, the emotion. It was concrete. Real, even if only in my imagination. I reached for it, used it to pull myself out of the dark. It must've taken hours. Hours and days and weeks, but I kept climbing. My body grew stronger as I rose, first simply the idea of a body until it was a powerful thing, the body I'd honed from months of training. I could do this. The voice whispered encouragements, steadying me as I lost my footing, rallying me as I grew tired.

Then, light. There was a blinding light. I ran for it.

Pain rocked through my body. Agony. I was blind all over again. I wanted to sink into the darkness. Wanted to give up. It was worse than dying, worse than the silver. It was like every nerve cell in my body was under attack, screaming out with pain.

"I know it hurts, little wolf, but you need to push through it." The voice. My constant companion.

I can do this. I'd vowed not to run away, and I wasn't going to give in now. I fought against the pain, not running from it but shoving back against it. I wouldn't let it end like this. Even if I was going to be petrified, I wasn't going down without a fight.

And then I opened my eyes.

CHAPTER XXVI

"**O**H GOOD, YOU'RE AWAKE."

I bolted upright, startled by the voice. Not Cole's.

No, it belonged to the same stunning woman I'd caught just a flash of before. She wore the same dress, I assumed, since I'd only seen the flash of purple. The dress was magnificent, embroidered with amethysts all over the expensive, sleek fabric. But the dress paled in comparison to her face. She must've been the most beautiful woman I'd ever seen, with full lips, sleek black hair that tumbled down her shoulders in endless curls, and eyes of deep violet.

I'd have appreciated it more if it didn't feel like someone was pounding my head with a sledgehammer.

"Where am I?"

The room was entirely unfamiliar. Instead of the simple stone of Cole's castle, the walls were covered in tapestries. Abstract swirls of colors. Cool, vibrant shades. Everything in the room was plush, from the settee the woman sat on to the bed, where I was propped up on a dozen overfull throw pillows.

I didn't want to spend another second in bed, but where to go? The room to the door was shut, and the woman was positioned between it and me. Maybe I could make a run for it, but I wasn't sure if this woman—witch, I remembered Cole saying distantly—was a threat.

"And who are you?" I added when the woman didn't immediately answer.

She smiled. It was a beautiful thing, like the rest of her. Yet it felt more like a viper flashing its fangs.

"You may call me Hecate," the witch said at last. "You're in one of my spare rooms, recovering from what threatened to be a nasty case of petrification. And I'd caution you, the next time you're tempted to turn to stone, pick something simple like a basilisk or cockatrice. Medusa's handiwork is a royal pain to deal with, even for me."

"Sure thing," I grumbled. Not that there'd ever be a repeat of that.

My headache started to recede. Hecate said nothing, continuing to sit next to the bed, observing me. Her posture was impeccable, whereas I was struggling to stay upright.

"Where's Cole?" I glanced to the door again as if expecting to see him. For some reason, I'd thought he'd stay with me.

Stupid. I should just count myself lucky he'd saved me from dying again—no, from a fate worse than death.

And I am totally going to need to tell him to get rid of the creepy statues.

"You'll see him at dinner."

I ground my teeth, not liking being denied access to Cole. Who was she to decide that?

Then again, she was the woman who'd saved my life. Maybe I should hold back on growling.

"This was, of course, the price he agreed to." Hecate rose from her chair in one elegant motion and then gestured to the other side of the room. "We'll dine in three-quarters of an hour. Please avail yourself of the facilities. I assure you everything will be to your satisfaction."

She left the room with a flourish, practically floating across the floor before the door magically shut behind her. Meanwhile, when I went to roll myself off the bed, I immediately collapsed, like my muscles were unused to working together.

Ugh.

I forced myself to stand, stumbling like a newborn deer, and reached the door Hecate had just walked out of. It didn't budge. I summoned my shifter strength, trying again. The handle didn't so much as jiggle. I gave one final yank with everything I had. It started to give, bending half an inch.

Green sparks flew from the handle. I jumped back.

I was stuck here. I weighed my options. Sure, I could yell, try to get someone's attention, but I reconsidered. Cole had trusted the witch enough to heal me. I couldn't outdo the magic. I might as well "avail myself" and be done with it.

The door she'd pointed to led to a bathroom that was easily the size of the bedroom. A massive, claw-foot tub sat filled with steaming hot water and rose petals greeted me. Suddenly, I was acutely aware of the general icky feeling over my skin. Considering I'd been halfway to turning into stone, that wasn't entirely unexpected. I shucked off what remained of my clothing and submerged myself in the water.

After twenty minutes of scrubbing every inch of my skin with another rose-scented soap, I felt almost like myself. Getting out of the tub required minimal effort. My body was quickly recovering from the after-effects of Medusa's gaze.

A large, fluffy towel appeared on the edge of the tub. I frowned for a second. Despite the fact I turned into a wolf with regular ease, the magic unnerved me. Shifting was one thing. Normal. Natural. Towels popping up? Weird.

I dried myself off and stepped in front of the mirror so I could run my hands through my tangle of red curls. The bathroom counter included everything I could ever want, from combs to perfume to makeup. Nothing like what I'd encountered in Cole's castle.

Something clawed in my throat as I thought of him. *Where was that black wolf?*

I forced myself to focus on getting dressed. I considered ignoring the makeup altogether, but it was such a rarity I let myself indulge in the basics, eyeliner, mascara, and lipstick. Daphne would be proud. There hadn't been much point dressing up in Moon-Ghost, at least for me, but why not? I had time to kill since that stupid door was unlikely to open a minute before the witch intended.

Once satisfied by my mediocre job at prettying myself, it was time to get dressed. I was pretty sure some of those gray splatters on my discarded clothes were Medusa's guts. It was more tempting to keep the towel than to put them back on.

My internal debate was solved not even a second later when my gaze snagged on a dress hanging off the wall. That *definitely* hadn't been there before.

It was a scarlet red gown, cut low in the front and built to cling to every curve. Not my usual tank top and sweatpants combo, but it was that or gut-covered clothing, so I snagged the dress off its perch and tried it on. I couldn't see myself fully in the mirror, but what I saw was enough. The dress fit perfectly, hugging every inch of my body like it was made for me.

In fairness, it probably was.

The woman in the mirror looked foreign to me. My skin looked brighter, my features fitting my face better. In Moon-Ghost, I'd had to sneak every scrap of food. I'd been weak. Now, my body was made of muscle, my skinny angles turned into curves that the dress highlighted. With makeup, I could almost call myself pretty.

Yeah, because that was something I should be focusing on after nearly having died and being trapped in a witch's castle with no way out.

I exited the bathroom and saw a pair of six-inch heels. Deep red to match the dress. I grimaced. No way. If I needed to make a run for it, those things would make sure I snapped my neck trying to get away. Besides, the gown barely grazed the floor as it was.

I tried the door again, and it opened.

Guess it's time for dinner.

CHAPTER XXVII

I FOUND MY WAY to the dining room the way any self-respecting shifter would: with my nose.

A dozen different scents rolled through the halls. My stomach growled in response.

It took only a few minutes to stride through the halls and enter the massive dining hall. Hecate sat in the middle of a long table, fit to seat at least thirty, with mounds of food atop it.

And Cole sat at the head.

He looked... different. His wild hair was brushed back. His clothes, while not entirely as fancy as my own, were suitable for a dinner party, with a black silk shirt and jacket completing the ensemble. He turned when I entered the room. A flash of relief crashed across his face as he took me in. *Maybe he did care a smidge, even if he wasn't there when I woke up.*

As he took in my appearance, his expression turned almost... wolfish. My steps faltered at that look. My mind immediately slid back to the kiss in the woods. The way he'd tasted. The way he'd felt.

The way I wanted him even now.

"I told you she was well," Hecate reassured him, breaking the silence. Her voice was like a gentle breeze, soft, feminine, unimposing.

There was something familiar in it when she spoke to Cole. I resisted the urge to flash my teeth at her. The two of them had history, yet he'd never mentioned her. Never mentioned anyone. Were they friends? Confidants? Lovers?

"Please, sit," she said, turning her soft, lilting voice to me.

I took a step towards Cole. Hecate cut me off with a discrete gesture to the other end of the table.

Odd. In our pack, the two ends of the table were reserved for the Alpha pair, the Beta, and the heir sitting at the right hand of either. For the first time in a while, the fleeting thought of my moon-matched mate didn't sting. It didn't feel like anything.

I wanted to be closer to Cole. Was tempted to continue and ignore her outstretched arm entirely.

But she had saved my life. I could play nice for one dinner.

I took my seat on the tall chair opposite Cole.

The second I sat, food moved about in a flurry, with several heaping servings of food making their way onto my plate. The roast ham cut itself into tidy portions, the roasted potatoes formed a neat mound, and the salad formed a minimally invasive tornado of leaves and tomatoes until we each had a full plate. My once empty glass was suddenly full of an aromatic red wine.

"Please, eat," Hecate said.

Not one to argue on this specific matter, I dug in. I was starving, hungrier than I'd been in ages. It was only when I was halfway through that I bothered to notice the lack of conversation.

I took a long sip of wine and stared as the glass refilled itself.

"Are you doing this, or is the glass magical?" I asked, raising my full glass to Hecate.

"That's a trick question, I suppose," the witch mused. "The glass is magical because I made it so. Before I enchanted it, it was nothing but a bit of melted sand."

I frowned. "Is that how everything works?" I glanced over the table at Cole. "Like the kitchen at your castle?"

"She's been to the castle?" Hecate asked, sounding surprised.

Cole ignored her. "That room was enchanted. The whole building was."

I chewed on a piece of ham, considering. I'd just accepted that some things were magical in the castle, but apparently, someone had done it. "Did you do that?"

"No, I'm afraid I can't take credit," Hecate said with modesty that somehow rang false.

We ate in silence for another moment, but more questions burned inside me.

"Were you always... magical?" I asked, unsure how to

phrase the question.

Hecate, thankfully, understood what I meant. "I've always had an aptitude, you could say. Curses are my forte, but I've had thousands of years to hone my craft so, at this point, differences are minimal. Many people have a magical spark. Of course, without training, you're liable to never properly control your magic or even realize it's there. I could train you if you wish."

I blinked, stunned. *Thousands of years?*

"I'm training her," Cole immediately growled.

"You were always hopeless at the arcane arts." Hecate dismissed him with wave of her hand.

"I don't have magic," I interrupted. "I'm just a shifter. Like Cole." Unless he was keeping more secrets.

Scratch that. He was definitely keeping more secrets.

Hecate laughed. "Of course you have magic. You've simply failed to notice. Think back. How'd you chase off the Taurus demon? Or push *him* off you? Or turn the knob of my enchanted door? All those things require magic."

"Spying?" Cole ground out the word like it was a shard of broken glass.

"Scrying," Hecate corrected without a care.

I thought back to the green sparks. I'd ignored them or assumed they came from something else. Had they really come from *me?*

"Don't you want to master your magic? It's the only reason

you're still alive."

"Pretty sure I'm quite dead," I quipped, still trying to process everything the witch had said.

"Enough." The command in Cole's voice left no room for argument. "I agreed to dinner. Not a lecture."

"It's not a lecture, it's someone giving me answers you clearly haven't," I snapped at the wolf across from me.

He fixed his amber eyes on me. Hit me with every inch of that Alpha stare. I refused to look away. Refused to back down. "Did you know?" I demanded, rising from my seat. My hands curled into fists.

"The things I know fill libraries," Cole shot back, rising to match me.

"And mine, cities," Hecate said mildly. "But there's no need to turn my dining table into a sparring ring."

A moment passed, and we both sank back into our chairs to finish the dinner in silence. When we finished, the food vanished as if by silent command. We stood and made our way to the front of the halls, the tension palpable between Cole and me. Hecate, for her part, seemed utterly serene.

"Before I forget, there's an... item for you in the southwest hall," she told Cole.

I furrowed my brow. Why wouldn't she just magic it over to us the way she did everything else? Cole gave a look that I thought conveyed a similar sentiment, but he didn't argue. A rarity for him.

Curiosity gnawed at me while we waited by the entrance. Two massive panels of gold made up the gateway to Hecate's domain. More than simple metal, they were engraved with sweeping images. Wolves, the moon, stars, rivers, mountains. With a flick of her wrist, the metal creaked.

"Thanks for healing me," I said as the palatial doors parted to open.

"My pleasure," Hecate said, sounding almost genuine. "It's not every day that someone as important as the king of the underworld makes a request of me."

I froze. King?

No. No, no, no. Cole couldn't be the king of anything.

It had to be an expression. Or something. My brain went into overdrive, a thousand half-formed defenses and justifications. There was no way Cole had kept something like that from me.

"That's a joke, right? I mean, he has a castle and all, but it's always empty."

Hecate blinked. "Oh yes, that. That's his... what would the mortal term be? Vacation home," she settled on.

What the *actual* Hell?

Chapter XXVIII

"His real castle is in the capital city, naturally."

Naturally.

How had I not known any of this? Even now, I had no idea what it meant. Cole was the king of Hell? Cole, the arrogant bastard who lazed around in silk sheets and spent hours training me each day, who had a dungeon in his "vacation home" and barely alive statues and a magic kitchen?

She had to be joking.

There was no way. Absolutely no way.

No way it could be true, yet I was only now finding out.

"That's enough," Cole snarled, suddenly reappearing.

I expected a denial. A punchline.

One look at him told me everything I needed to know.

Betrayal lit through me. Disgust at myself for my ignorance. And somehow, even under that, jealousy. Jealous that this witch, who I'd never heard of, knew that Cole had a castle. That he could get to the capital city. That he ruled this realm.

If he wanted to, he could've helped me get back to the mortal realm at any time, probably.

I turned away from him.

"Avery." My name. Not little wolf. A warning? An apology?

I said nothing.

"Thank you again for all your help," Cole growled. This wasn't directed at me. Still, I didn't look at him.

The trip back to the castle was silent. I couldn't even formulate a single question to sum up the thoughts ricocheting through my head. It was only when we finally reached the drawbridge, and the warmth of the lava filled my skin, that I paused.

Cole looked back, expectant.

"Is it true?" I asked quietly.

He lifted his amber eyes to my green ones. Held them for a moment.

Then he turned back to the entrance, throwing the door wide. "We train tomorrow at dawn."

For Cole, the matter was closed after that. The next days were uneventful, but there was no ease to them. Cole was keeping major secrets, and the visit to Hecate was bitter medicine.

A reminder that Cole was not my alpha. Not my packmate. Not my anything. Was I grateful I hadn't been turned to stone forever? Yes.

But there were so many questions, and Cole refused all of them. Who he was, how to get to the city, why Hecate referred to him that way. I railed at him until I was hoarse, but he refused any answers. "I'll tell you when you beat me," was his constant refrain.

It was like he was shoving me away. The library was fruitless. I turned my search to books on magic, but it was hard to tell what was real and what was fabricated. There was no mention of the green sparks I sometimes summoned.

We were still meeting in the mornings to train, but it was brief. Perfunctory. All of two hours, and then we'd escape to our corners of the castle—the "vacation home" Hecate had called it. There was nothing to do but spend time reading. The library had been my refuge before, but now I spent almost all my time there.

Today, I'd settled again in my usual chair, having decorated it with a smattering of books on the floor, arms, and even bent open over the back of the chair.

Cole entered. Normally, he left me alone in the afternoons. I sensed his entrance immediately. I hated the way I was attuned to his movements. My once dull senses were sharp to his presence. I kept telling myself it was just because he was the only one I was able to spend time around.

He didn't stride over to me. I refused to look up at him. The words on the book in front of me—a field guide to the flora of some far-off realm—turned into jumbled letters. I must've read the same sentence five times without gaining its meaning. I bit back a growl of frustration.

"You like the library." A statement, but perhaps an invitation for conversation.

Maybe because it might give me the answers you won't, I wanted to snarl, but at the same time, part of me was tired of fighting with Cole. Of course, I didn't want to roll over. All secrets were not forgiven.

"Yes," was the answer I settled on.

I wasn't sure why he was here. Had he come for a book? He was looking at me. I could feel it on the back of my neck. Maybe one of mine? I surveyed what I had sprawled in front of me. Initially, I'd worked hard to put the books I took off the shelf back. Now, I'd slowly built towers of them. Not to mention the stacks I kept in my room.

The field guide failed to recapture my interest. I finally tossed it aside and looked at him. He was leaning against a stack of nearby shelves, surveying me. I decided to look back, my gaze wary. Part of me craved to be near him. The part that rolled over, belly up, whenever I shifted. But that was just my loneliness. I'd take anyone. For so long, I'd had just Daphne. *There* was someone who'd earned my loyalty time and time again, someone who didn't keep secrets.

His brows knit up, a flash then gone, as he saw what I'd been reading. Not the most exciting read, but I didn't need him judging my reading preferences. It had been kind of interesting before he'd entered the library and ruined my peace.

I tried to rationalize the betrayal. He owed me nothing.

He was doing more for me than he needed to. He—or, well, Hecate—had saved my life. I replayed my conversation with the witch over and over, trying to decipher every hidden meaning.

But, moon, it stung.

Finally, I couldn't take the silence anymore. "Do you have magic?" I asked. It was one of the dozen questions that had been floating through my head.

I could practically feel Cole weighing his words. "Not like you." An answer that wasn't really an answer. Surprise.

But it was also a challenge. A test. To see what I'd do with that scrap of information.

Well, it just made me hungry for me. "How can I have magic?"

"The same way anyone does. Being born with it."

"I didn't have magic when I was alive, though," I argued.

"How can you be sure?" he asked.

Of course I didn't have magic. Not beyond whatever let us turn to wolves at will, and even that had always been weak. "I never felt anything like Hecate mentioned when I was alive."

"Your body could barely handle shifting by your own admission," Cole said, as if psychically able to pick up where my thoughts had gone. Magic, or did he simply know me? *Which was worse?* "Since coming here, you've become a hundred times more powerful. Isn't it possible other skills were amplified?"

I tried to keep the surprise off my face. Well, in Hell, the impossible was possible. Maybe here I could be powerful.

I stood from my chair. There were many types of power. Since training with Cole, I'd claimed one.

He stayed where he was, leaning against the shelves. But his gaze was on me. I was acutely aware of the fact I was still in my workout gear from this morning. Spandex shorts and a sports bra. I'd worn it with a loose top when we'd trained this morning, a top I discarded once we went off on our own, back inside.

But here I was. Exposed. Skin bared. I'd told myself before Cole didn't even notice me. He'd been so careful to keep locked up that side of him that had greeted me the first day. On the occasions I thought back to it, he seemed like a different male that day. Hedonistic, seductive, unconcerned. Unlike the hard ass who trained me, relentlessly, day in, day out. The one who gave cryptic answers because I didn't deserve real answers in his eyes.

But I'd had a glimpse of the other male. The one who pressed me against a tree and kissed me. The one who made my pulse race, not from fear or fury but raw desire. Desire he'd matched.

I moved towards Cole, slow. His pupils dilated just slightly, taking in the sway of my hips, but there was a hint of caution.

"Cole." I was a step away from him now. Still, he hadn't moved. His arms were crossed over his chest, a neutral, easy pose.

Yet my shifter senses were sharp. Sharp in a way they'd never been above ground. I could taste emotions on my tongue if I focused enough.

"Little wolf," was his easy reply.

And when I stood in front of him, defiant, curve-hugging clothes leaving me exposed a foot from him, I could taste that the male wanted me.

"I want to train with Hecate."

Chapter XXIX

I'd expected Cole to tell me no. I'd expected an argument.

But perhaps he felt some lingering shade of guilt for all the secrets because he simply looked at me for a moment. Not at my body or behind me. He held my gaze, not in challenge but like he was trying to see inside my head.

"If that's what you wish."

That was how a few days later, I wound up at Hecate's palace. There was no other word for the building now that I'd had a chance to properly see it. The witch had shooed Cole off, offering a hundred promises that I'd be perfectly fine. She said it so many times I started to wonder if I had something to worry about, honestly.

Hecate was beautifully dressed, like last time, with layers of gossamer midnight blue cloth covering her body. Her hair caught the light with ease, capturing it in dark strands, yet her pale skin seemed nearly ghostly. She was utterly composed, even while assuring Cole I wouldn't disappear in a poof of smoke.

Whatever I'd been prepared for on the first day, it hadn't been to go back to school. Hecate led me to an impossibly lovely indoor garden with a small waterfall built inside it. I saw several impossible things I was forced to accept.

"How do we start bibbity-bobbity-booing?" I asked, bouncing on the balls of my feet. If I could do magic like they both said, then I was eager to harness it.

Hecate fixed me with a look. Her expression didn't so much as twitch, her flawless face polite, yet I felt chastised all the same.

"We start by giving you a proper foundation, Soteria."

I frowned. She'd saved my life and didn't even know my name? "Uh, it's Avery, actually," I corrected.

A dismissive wave. "Of course I know your name. Now, sit, Soteria."

I decided against arguing since I did want to learn magic, and at least it wasn't as condescending as Cole's *little wolf* moniker. I turned around to look for a place to sit, and a school desk and chair appeared. It was old-fashioned, not like what we'd had at the pack school, but closer to something from an old cartoon, with a curved back seat and simple tilted surface. I sat.

A chalkboard magically appeared four feet in front of me in the garden. Hecate already had the chalk in hand, and she wasted no time beginning to teach.

Just like that, I was back in school.

At the end of the first day, I thought my brain was going to fall out of my ears, it was so overfull with magical knowledge. Hecate was an excellent teacher, but most of what she said seemed impossible to grasp. I left weary but craving more. I stayed up late at night, combing through books in the library that matched what she'd talked about. After the second day, she gave me a book from her own library.

I poured myself into those books and lessons. If only to have a break from everything said and unsaid with Cole. Each day, he escorted me to Hecate's building, then returned in the evening to take me back. We didn't share meals anymore. Some days I ate with the witch, others I grabbed a snack from the ever-full kitchen after returning, Cole nowhere to be found.

"Is it making sense?" Hecate asked, a week into lessons.

"Not really," I admitted. Hecate had explained the concept twice over now—today's subject was the connection between a person and their inner magic's form. The way her forte was curses, though now she could charm, enchant, teleport, and many more things.

I'd asked her about the teleportation days ago. Unfortunately, it was no good for intra-realm travel, she told me.

I could repeat back the concept in different words, but it just wasn't clicking. "I get that some people are going to be more talented in some areas, I just don't see how you can know which exact one it is, aside from trying everything and seeing what works the best."

Hecate shook her head, the waterfall of raven hair swaying. "It's not a matter of talent. It's a matter of the innate shape your magic takes when it reaches out before you consciously do anything else."

"Like the green sparks?" I asked.

"Not quite," the witch said. She gestured for me to follow her through the garden. I stood from my seat. It and the desk I'd been working at promptly disappeared in that instant way I'd come to expect. I caught my notebook that had been resting on the desk before it hit the ground. "Look around you. What do you see?"

I glanced through the luscious space. "Plants, mostly. Flowers, trees, grass." The term garden didn't quite due justice to the inner courtyard of the witch's palace.

Hecate drew me over to a bush of roses, large red blossoms. She selected one from the tangle of branches and held it out to me without severing the stem.

"It's a rose," I said dumbly.

She flicked her wrist. The rose was gone, transformed. "Now it's a peony."

Hecate shook her head. "No. It was always a rose, but I can force it to change." The peony turned back to a rose. Another twist of her fingers and the blossom turned gray, ashen, and crumbled into dust on the ground. Only the thorn-covered stem remained. "The same way my magic wants to curse the flower, but I can force it to transform instead. I am excellent at being a transmoglifier. But I'm a curser. Each time, I tame the magic to do what I wish. Do you understand now?"

I nodded. "I think so."

"Then see what you do to this." She extended another stem to me. Unlike the perfectly blooming blossom before, this was a small bud, barely open.

I held it. Stared at it. Willed it to do something.

The rose was unimpressed. As was my teacher.

She placed a gentle yet firm hand on my shoulder, forcing it to relax. "Stop trying so hard. When you change into your wolf, do you think about it? Do you crease your brow so hard you have wrinkles to rival a crone's? Or do you simply let your soul stretch into the shape it wishes?"

"But... I've always been a shifter," I argued.

"And you've always been a witch."

I closed my eyes, taking a breath, escaping the pressure of her violet gaze. Inhaled the rose's scent as I breathed in. Loosed the tension as I exhaled. Forced myself to relax, to chase out the thoughts of what I should be doing. I centered only on those green sparks, trying to summon them the way I summoned the shift. Not with a conscious thought of breaking and reforming every bone in my body and growing fur and claws, but letting instinct take over.

"Now look," Hecate said quietly.

I opened my eyes. A flicker of a green spark faded, leaving

the flower in front of me. The bud had... bloomed. As beautiful and full as the rose she'd turned to dust. I spun to look at her. "How?"

She smiled. "Magic, of course."

CHAPTER XXX

A FTER MAKING THE ROSE bloom, I kind of figured the lessons would get easier. Things would make sense, and I'd be slinging spells like Hecate in no time.

Ha.

Ha.

No.

The lessons still included lectures at the magical chalkboard—the chalk doing the writing on its own while Hecate gestured—but with the added bonus of practical lessons after.

"The flower was a fluke," I said with a growl as I failed another practical lesson. I'd been able to grasp the concepts better after that one success, but I was growing doubtful I could manage something like that again.

"It was not." Hecate, to her credit, never lost patience with my many failures. Each day, she assured me I did have the talent, it was simply a matter of training myself to use them. "You've lived your life with your physical senses—scent, sight, and so on. It's just a matter of reconnecting your sense of magic."

I nodded and tried once more at the task. There was an unlit candle in front of me. My task was simple, obvious.

I couldn't even get the green sparks to show up. I slumped down, disappointed.

I'd been used to being a failure my whole life. I'd lived as the pack Omega. Unable to shift with any strength. Scrawny. Vulnerable. It was never a surprise when my bullies went after me and I once again lost.

But here, I'd let myself believe I could be strong. As a shifter, I was confident I could take on any member of the Alpha clique, except maybe Jett—who I avoided thinking about. My moon-matched, murderous mate.

Being killed by him had been another cruel blow, surprising in that he'd been assigned to me by fate, but not in the fact he'd wanted me dead and been able to triumph over me.

Those memories were so distant most days. But my failures with Hecate brought them back. I was finally a decent shifter, but I was a pathetic witch.

"You simply lack the right motivation," Hecate said. "Come. We will try something different."

Aside from the one dinner, I hadn't seen much of the castle outside of the same path we walked each day into the center courtyard. She led me farther inside to a winding staircase that went down. For a half-second, I froze, remembering my trip to Cole's dungeon.

"Uh, if your plan is to throw a murderous creature at me and see if I defend myself with magic, I would like to veto that plan," I said hesitantly.

"Veto?" Hecate said, continuing down the stairs.

I followed her despite my initial hesitation. "Nix. Reject. Take off the table."

"Mm-hmm." Hecate's heels clicked on the stone.

Well, can't blame a wolf for trying. I granted myself a moment of distraction, remembering what Cole had done. I expected the burn of anger at how he'd gone about it. Instead, a different burn went through me. Late at night, I could almost taste his demanding kiss on my lips, feel the way he'd pressed me against the tree.

The thought kept me in a distracted cloud until I realized we'd reached the bottom.

We were definitely underground. Hecate had led me to a large cavern, though it was more a cave than a room built of stone blocks. Torches periodically dotted the wall, granting just enough light for my wolf vision to make out the contents of the room.

In the center was a small pool. No, I realized as Hecate and I walked towards it. A basin. A massive bowl, maybe eight feet by eight, held up by a claw-foot platform.

"This is a scrying mirror. It's used to see others," Hecate explained.

"Um, cool," I said. "How does it work?"

"You'll see."

I frowned. "I kind of haven't been successful at the simple stuff. I'm not sure this will go any better."

"Scrying taps into a different part of your psyche than the candle," Hecate said. "The candle is simple power, manifested. Scrying is driven by desire. You will see what—or more accurately, who—you wish in the pool. Look in its depths."

I looked into the water. My reflection looked back. I tried to reign in my skepticism, but it was hard. Not that Hecate was right. More that I'd be able to do whatever she was talking about.

"Look farther, Soteria. Not at the surface, but see beyond. Think of someone. Someone important. Let the emotion guide your sight."

I looked and then looked some more. *Desire.*

The word stirred one thought. *Cole.*

His hands on me. His demanding mouth. The way he looked at me like he wanted to throttle me when training. The way he smelled when he wanted me.

My reflection faded away. The water grew dark. For a second, I thought it was broken. Then, a figure emerged from the murky water. Dark hair, large stature, and distinctive amber eyes that seemed to look through the water at me. He was standing out somewhere, a lake behind him that I thought I'd seen once when I'd first come, surveying the area. I couldn't see what he was looking at, though. Instead, he seemed nearly in front of me.

He turned slightly, as if to face me. I jumped away from the water.

"Can he see us?"

"Most individuals cannot sense if they're being scried upon. But Cole is likely aware some form of magic is present around him." Once again, I wanted to know just what he was. How powerful he was. Cole was clearly an alpha, but he was so much more, as Hecate hinted at.

"Now, try again. Focus on a person, and then see them. Let your feelings guide your magic rather than conscious effort."

My mind turned away from Cole on the second attempt. Instead, I pictured my friend. Daphne Gallagher. The one wolf in Moon-Ghost who hadn't scorned me. The one whose scent made me feel like I was home with a sibling I'd never had. I let myself remember our times together. Doing each other's hair in her bedroom. Finding random corners of the school to hide and eat lunch in. Driving to the Choosing together, talking about all the possibilities the future held. It had been the last time I'd seen her... had she met her own moon-matched mate? Was she well? Did she grieve me? I was sure she did, yet I wanted her to find happiness.

Grief of my own washed over me, more melancholy than sharp. Because she was surely okay, and though I was dead, I was still, in a way, alive. But she didn't know. There was a veil of life and death dividing us.

For a moment, I sank into the feeling. Then, I looked down into the basin.

The image that emerged was first focused on her face, like a zoomed-in picture. I could make out the beauty mark under her right eye. The curly strands of blonde hair she normally straightened framed her face. She was lying down, asleep.

The image moved out, letting me see more. I frowned. She was asleep, but not in her bed. Not in pajamas. At least not her usual. Daphne had always been very pro-matching sets of PJs. But this was a dirty, ratty T-shirt. She had an old, thin blanket on her, covering the rest of her body.

But she wasn't in a bed.

No, the image moved out farther, and I finally placed where she was.

She was in a Moon-Ghost cell.

Chapter XXXI

"**T**HIS CAN'T BE RIGHT," I stammered. "I must've done something wrong."

"Why do you believe so?" Hecate inquired.

I looked at the image in front of me. It rippled as fear gripped me, but I chased it away, trying to remain focused on Daphne. The water stilled again, and my heart lurched. "That's my best friend. She wasn't an outcast like me. Her parents are respected in the pack. They wouldn't just put her in a cell."

I looked closer and noticed more details—the dirtiness of her hair, the thinness of her cheeks, her hollow collar. This was a mistake. It had to be.

Hecate stood next to me, looking down at the image. She waved a hand over it, and I would swear I could feel her magic pulse against my skin. "You've done nothing wrong. The image is as the truth is."

I growled. "You're telling me she's really locked up?"

"Yes."

I swallowed. How could they do this to her? Sweet, funny

Daphne. I turned to Hecate. "We have to do something. I can't leave her like this." In all the times I'd been bullied, beaten, and shoved in some cramped locker, Daphne had never abandoned me.

"There is nothing you can do from here," Hecate said, her voice calm but sympathetic.

"There must be something! If I can magically see her from here, then you can cast a spell to help her. To set her free. Help her escape."

"Scrying is but a window that lets you look through. You cannot use magic between realms, unfortunately."

"There has to be a way," I insisted. Pleaded. Seeing my closest friend in that condition was a physical pain. The sting of failure blended with heartache. "You said there's nothing that can be done from here, but what if I went back?" I'd slowly given up my quest to return. I'd gotten no closer to any real answers in the library, but Hecate had to know something. "I read a book about portals. Libra demons control them, right?"

Hecate hesitated. "Perhaps this is something you would be better served discussing with Cole, Soteria."

But I can't trust Cole. My inner wolf whined at the thought, but he'd been keeping this knowledge from me, plus all his other secrets. He wouldn't tell me. "Please, Hecate. She's my best friend." She wavered. "Tell me if I'm right, at least. Can a Libra demon take me back to the realm of the living so I can help Daphne?"

A pause. I chewed on the inside of my cheek, trying not to press Hecate too far, but I was desperate.

"Yes," she admitted at last.

"Then tell me how to find one." If I could find one, I could beg, bargain, or just thrash the demon into agreeing to take me. Whatever it took.

"Soteria, I must again suggest you discuss how to do this with your... *host*."

I knew deep in my bones what Cole's reaction to that would be. Yes, he had agreed to let me train with Hecate, even though he didn't like it. But Cole never did anything unless he wanted to, and he'd made his terms of me figuring out this information clear—I'd have to beat him in a fight. I could train with Hecate and him both for another year and still not succeed. "You know as well as I do he'd never go for it."

"No, he would not let you go," Hecate reluctantly agreed. "Not as you are now."

"Then tell me how," I begged.

Hecate sighed. "Very well. You must go to the capital. I will tell you how. But I warn you, you may not like what you find."

C OLE RETURNED TO ESCORT me back shortly after. He did this every day, even though it was completely unnecessary. After the second day, I'd memorized the route. There were no demons to speak of. But for whatever reason, I never told him to stop doing it.

Despite the time we spent together on the journey, we didn't speak. I didn't even know what to say to him, but if I was going to get to Daphne, I was going to need to.

Anxiety thrummed through me. Part of it was due to Daphne. But the other half was driven by the knowledge of what I would have to do to rescue her. Do to Cole.

"You were spying on me," Cole said, breaking the silence. The words, which could've been accusatory, were neutral. An opening.

I'd been so lost in my thoughts that his voice momentarily startled me. "Scrying," I corrected, channeling Hecate.

"Your lessons must be going well, then."

"'Well' might be a stretch," I admitted. "Plus, it was only for a minute, really." I avoided mentioning my second attempt that had led me to Daphne. Plus, it wasn't really a lie. Aside from the slight success today, I'd failed at nearly every other task the witch had given me.

"You'll master it all in time." The confidence in his voice was a balm to my wounded ego. He sounded so sure. It made me want to believe him.

"Like I mastered being a shifter?" I snorted.

"Patience, little wolf. You can't master all the arcane arts in a handful of afternoons."

I huffed, but his words were comforting nonetheless.

It made me feel bad for what I was planning to do.

For a moment, I considered confiding in Cole. Yes, he kept secrets. But he'd helped me time and time again. Deep in my soul, I wanted to trust him. I wanted to let the wolf decide. But I couldn't risk it. Couldn't risk telling him and being shut down again, denied assistance—or worse, having him stop me.

I had only ever truly been able to rely on one person—myself. Daphne hadn't saved me from everything, but she'd been my friend for years.

And I would fall to any depths to rescue her in turn.

Even if that meant betraying the male I felt more drawn to than I had any right to.

"Hecate gave me this for dessert," I said, hefting an aromatic parcel. It was a delicious, fresh pie. I was pretty sure it hadn't existed before I'd asked Hecate to conjure it two hours ago. The sweet smell filled my wolf senses.

I hoped it succeeded in covering the scents of the plants I'd sneaked from Hecate's garden that were pressed against my skin.

"Maybe we can have it with dinner," I said, tentative.

It was a gamble. We'd largely been avoiding each other, taking our meals separately. If Cole declined, my plan wouldn't work.

When Cole nodded, I had to fight the exhale of relief that

threatened to leave my body. I wasn't out of the woods—or Hell—yet.

"I'll meet you in three hours," the male said.

I agreed. We'd reached the castle, and I split off to my room. Three hours might seem like a long time, but I had a lot to prepare before then. I returned to my room, allowing the door to shut softly before tearing across the space. I tossed books away, searching for the one I knew I'd taken weeks ago. From when I'd started going to the library and taking whatever books caught my fancy.

Phytotoxicology.

The study of poison plants.

I emptied the plants I'd grabbed from Hecate's garden from my clothes and quickly rinsed my skin of the toxins. The plants—particularly the aconitum—were unpleasant individually, but I'd need to mix them together to accomplish my task. The book was relatively straightforward, aside from the language. The recipe called for mortar and pestle to mix the plants, but I settled for grinding them between the stone floor and a dish I'd taken from the kitchen the other day and hadn't yet returned.

First, the aconitum with nightshade formed the base. A few other herbs Hecate had helped me identify were ground in smaller quantities. They had to be so fine all the particles were effectively indistinguishable, even to my eyes. Finally, a few red flower seeds, which turned the powder a dark red. I tore a blank page from a book and collected it from the floor, gathering the detritus and hiding it in the back of my closet. The scent wasn't too pungent, but we were wolves. I couldn't risk Cole figuring out what I was doing.

I couldn't let myself guess what he would do if he discovered my plan.

The nixie had been just one example of his lethality. And that hadn't been personal.

By my guess, dinner was another hour away once I finished. I changed into fresh clothes. An odd, girlish part of me wanted to dress up for dinner. The clothes that magically appeared certainly accommodated. I could wear a dress like the one I'd worn at that dinner with Hecate.

I could make him look at me that way. The way that turned my skin electric. That made me want to run my claws down his back.

But I had to be practical. This wasn't a... a *date*. And yet, my plan did hinge on him being distracted.

Maybe it wasn't so impractical to dress up after all.

I didn't go for a ball gown. Odds were, I'd need to shift before the night was done, making the question of clothing moot. But I'd need to move fast once I used the concoction. I wound up in a tight-fitting, long-sleeved shirt that stopped at my belly button, with a black miniskirt that showed off my toned legs. To think, months ago I'd been scrawny. If I went back to the land of the living, would I keep all these new developments? I'd grilled Hecate for the scant details she'd provided before leaving, and though she was uncertain, she believed I would. I should even be able to wield magic in the living realm, though if I couldn't do that in Hell—well, think snowball's chance.

All in all, my plan had maybe a thirty percent chance of working on Cole.

For the steps after, I'd dropped that to maybe five percent. I didn't have a clue what I was doing. I couldn't beat Cole in a fight, and I might be running into the arms of even worse than him.

Even if I succeeded, Cole would be angry. Furious.

There would be consequences.

But dammit, I had lived my life shying away from consequences, from fear, and where had that gotten me?

If I was going to piss someone off, well...

At least this time I'd do something to deserve it.

Chapter XXXII

THE KITCHEN WAS... DIFFERENT.

Not magically different in the way I was becoming accustomed to with Hecate, who would flick her wrist and transform our entire landscape. It was the same size, same scents. There was a table in the back, covered in an ornately embroidered purple cloth. It wasn't massive, not like the one at Hecate's. But it changed the space, turning the room we normally grabbed a quick bite into a proper dining room. The lighting was dim, the candles providing enough to see but not the all-illuminating brightness I was accustomed to.

But then Cole...

For a moment, when I saw him, that was all I could think. Not of my scheme or Daphne or even how to breathe. There was only Cole.

In the past months, he'd seemed allergic to so much as combing his hair, even though the wild look suited him. Now he looked like an aristocrat. He wore his customary black, but like me, he'd shed his sweats for proper clothing. The clothes must've been magically designed because he filled them perfectly. The collar of his shirt was open, revealing a hint of the muscles on his chest. The sleeves were rolled up, as if to make the look casual, but it was a far cry from our usual.

Cole assessed me the same way I did him. He might've been showing off a bit of muscle here and there, but I was on display. I should've done it because it was part of my plan.

But the truth was... a secret part of me just wanted him to look at me like that.

I should say something. The nerves I'd studiously ignored returned.

It had been easy to banter with Cole during training up until the kiss.

Now, I was off kilter. But I couldn't let him sense that. Couldn't give him a reason to suspect.

"You, err, don't look terrible." Avery Ward, master of flattery.

His eyes narrowed. "You're nervous."

Oops. He could smell it on me, no doubt.

Well, the best defense was a vigorous offense. "I just don't want to wind up pinned against a tree again," I huffed.

"And you're wearing that?" An arched brow. "I'll remind you, you did a fair bit of pinning yourself."

"Only because I was trying to throttle you," I argued, taking a step forward.

The grin that broke across Cole's face was nothing short of devilish. "By all means, throttle away."

"Maybe I'll just choke you next time."

"I think you just want an excuse to get your hands on me," Cole demurred.

Ugh! Infuriating male. "If by that you mean I want to shred you with my claws, sure."

"Kinky."

The word threw me off balance. Cole and I had met halfway without me even noticing it. He was there, towering over me, amber orbs looking down. Close enough for me to scent him deeply rather than the array of food spread out around us. I should be focused on my mission, yet I couldn't help but breathe him in. Desire. Want. Need. They warred through me.

"Actually, I'm hungry," I said, forcing myself to take a step back and walk around Cole to the table. Hecate's dessert, I noticed, was displayed in the center.

"If it's food you're hungry for, then by all means."

I *was* hungry. And nervous. The powder sat heavy, pressed between my chest. I needed Cole to ingest it. Hecate had been clear about how it worked. But there was no way for me to access the food.

We ate in silence for a moment. Maybe due to nerves, or maybe just because I wanted to be able to talk to Cole, I wound up recounting more of my lessons with Hecate. He listened with an intensity that made me self-conscious, but whenever I was about to stop, he'd urge me on with a question or insightful comment.

"For someone who claims to not do magic, you sure know a lot about it." I sighed.

A cocky smirk. "You don't get to be my age without knowing a few tricks."

"And how old is that again, Grandpa?" I was curious, oddly desperate for any scrap of information about Cole.

He considered for a moment. Once again weighing what information he'd be willing to part with. "Older than I can remember."

"And... you've been here this whole time? In Hell? In this castle?"

"Not exactly."

Cole apparently managed to fight his underwhelming urge to elaborate and left me with a frustratingly cryptic answer. I prodded a bit more, but he'd say no more. I stopped pushing because I got the sense Cole wasn't hiding information to be an asshole. Wherever he'd been before... it hadn't been pleasant.

"Hecate said this is your vacation home," I said, changing tactics.

"I was wondering when this would come up," was his response.

"So it's true?" I pushed.

He nodded. "After as long as I've spent in this realm, it would be odd to have only one residence, no?"

"I wouldn't really know. Not to brag, but I can actually remember how old I am." At least, I could for now. It was easy to lose track of the days down here. I'd spent mere months with Cole, but how soon would I lose count?

"How young." Unless I was crazy, there was a wistful note in Cole's voice.

"Not that young," I replied primly. "So, where's your other place? Why don't you ever go there?"

"This castle suits our—my purposes," Cole said, correcting himself and ignoring my first question.

It occurred to me I might actually get more answers from the stone statues Cole kept in the castle. Or banging his head against the castle walls and seeing what answers fell out that way.

Speaking of the creepy statues... "Why do you have all those statues? Are they all alive like... like I was?"

Cole didn't comment on my change in topic. "What would you have me do?"

"Can't Hecate fix them like she fixed me?"

Cole shook his head. "After this many eons, it's beyond even Hecate's powerful capabilities."

Eons? "How long was that crazy, snake-haired bitch in your dungeon, anyway? And why?" That was a question that had also plagued me.

Cole considered. "It took a century or so to secure her. As for the reason for her imprisonment, well, I should think it obvious."

"It's not," I argued. "Why not just kill her? Like you did… when you saved me?" It occurred to me I hadn't ever really thanked him for that.

He frowned. "What happens when one is killed in this realm is… beyond. It's not justice. It's cruel to sentence someone there when another option is available."

"You're telling me eternal imprisonment in Hell is preferable?"

"Undoubtedly."

Well, that wasn't promising. "Then why did you kill her? And the nixie?"

"I might have lost my temper," the male replied.

"So something is beyond Hecate," I mused. It was strange to think so, given how powerful the witch was. "How did you meet?"

A smile ghosted across his full lips. For a second, something raw and angry flared inside my chest. It took a breath to identify it as jealousy. I pushed it aside, determined to listen to his answer. He was actually sharing some information. And after my actions this evening, well, that might not happen again.

"Hecate was old when even I was young. I was arrogant when I came to this realm, and she quickly put me in my place."

I made my eyes go wide. "You? Arrogant? Say it ain't so."

That actually earned a gruff laugh from Cole. I found myself smiling at him. It was easy talking to him, I realized. Or at least, it could be.

But I was about to ruin it.

Chapter XXXIII

THE DINNER PROGRESSED. HECATE'S dessert was delicious, and as a bonus, neither of us turned into toads. Aside from providing the necessary herbs, she hadn't provided any mystical assistance. The dirty plates went away, and Cole and I wound up sipping wine. Rather, I was pretending to sip my wine. It was an effort to keep my nerves calm and prevent Cole from figuring out what I was planning.

No more procrastinating. It was time to turn my plan into reality. One way or another, Cole needed to get the concoction inside of him.

"You know, it's ironic," I said once the conversation lulled. "At one time, I would've given anything to avoid the Alpha clique and escape my old pack. And yet being tied to Jett is what freed me."

"You feel free here?"

"There's no comparison. There, I was weak. Picked on. I felt like I was fighting for my life every day, and it wasn't even close to a fair fight. But here, it's like I'm finally in control of my shifting. I mean, it's still dangerous here, but I feel like I have a fighting chance. And I'm learning, or trying to, some freaky magic. I'd call it an upgrade on all fronts." I realized it was true. If not for Daphne, I wouldn't ever dream of returning to my old life. Cole might not be a replacement for her—no one could replace her. But also, my feelings were different towards Cole. I didn't just want to think of him as a packmate. Even if I knew Cole could never regard me as an equal, could never see me as a real companion—sometimes, I thought he treated me more like a pet to be trained, fed, and kept alive—my shifter instincts demanded connection. Pack. Loyalty. If I'd had enough time, maybe, over the years, I really could've had that.

"That's certainly an optimistic take on Hell," Cole said, voice level.

"Well, it's not like I've seen much of Hell." It was dangerous territory I was edging towards.

Cole raised a brow as if to say, *This again?* I ignored it.

"I suppose if I asked for the grand tour you'd decline, huh?"

"What do you imagine you'd want a tour of?"

I tapped my fingers around my goblet. "Since this is your 'vacation home,' I suppose your main digs would be a good start. Just seems hospitable, right? I mean, why not? Hiding me from a wife?"

For a moment, a flash, Cole froze. Then he let out a light scoff. "I'll remind you that you let yourself into my 'vacation home.'"

"Hey, you're the one who wound up insisting I stay. If you're fed up with me, that's on you." I considered. "Though when I'd first shown up, you seemed... rather happy to see me. Or someone. I don't imagine you were expecting a wayward shifter to stumble into your bedroom."

"Only in my dreams," Cole said offhandedly.

"I used to have vivid dreams too," I confessed. "I was so lonely, I dreamed up these worlds and then had an imaginary friend I'd talk to. It sounds silly, but those dreams got me through a lot of rough days." I didn't know why I was sharing all of this. I'd never even told Daphne about the dreams. They were just dreams. I knew that. But they'd been so much more.

Then again, even if Cole thought it was stupid, what did it matter?

"That so." Not a question, though it was phrased as one. "And how many of your dreams starred me, little wolf?"

Involuntarily, I flushed, thinking back to the erotic dream I'd had a couple weeks ago. Fuck, that had felt real.

But it had just been a dream. Cole was heckling me, that weird taunting, teasing, flirting thing he did to throw me off-kilter.

Well, I could throw him right back.

"Oh, so many," I purred. "After we'd spar, I always needed a nap. Those things have an effect, you know?"

Cole regarded me, trying to figure out where I was going.

A small smile threatened my lips. "And we'd be so sweaty

from rolling around, you know? I'd have to toss my sweaty clothes right off before laying in bed… to nap, of course."

There it was, just the barest switch in his scent. Desire. It mirrored my own.

I continued, "And as I'd lay in bed, well, after some time, I'd fall asleep. And you'd be there. And we'd be rolling around, all sweaty." I kept my voice to a murmur, letting real emotions enter my words.

"And then?" Cole urged. His voice had grown husky.

"And then I'd straddle you… press against you…" Fuck, this shouldn't be affecting me too.

Cole loosed a soft growl.

"And then I'd roll us and pin you face down, grab the nearest object, and hit you until your stubborn ass cried uncle and told me whatever I wanted to know."

Cole blinked, taken aback by the turn it had taken. Then he laughed, a full bark of a laugh, and smiled.

The smile was more like bared teeth. "Violent little wolf."

I grinned back, matching him tooth for tooth. "You bring it out in me."

"You know I won't give you any answers until you can do that while *awake*."

I rolled my eyes. "Yeah, you've mentioned that a time or two." I dropped the sarcasm and asked seriously, "Do you really think I'll be able to best you? Or did you put an impossible challenge in front of me, never intending to give me the answers I want?"

Cole answered just as seriously. "You best me all the time, little wolf. You simply don't realize it." A pause. "But for the sparring... it's possible. Just not in the next year."

"You really don't want me going to find those demons." I sighed. There was no chance he'd help me if I'd asked him.

Cole's amber eyes flashed. "After all the work I've put into having you not die again, I'd rather avoid suicidal expeditions."

I didn't think he was giving me enough credit, but then again, how would I know? I'd only seen two demons. "Ever heard of the sunk cost fallacy?" I took a sip of my wine. "You're basically just saying you don't want to let me go because you've spent too much time training me to survive. It has nothing to do with me, Avery, as a person. It's just about the time and energy you put into a pet project."

Cole growled. "You're more than a *pet project.*"

"Am I?" I challenged.

"Isn't it obvious?"

From my expression, it *obviously* wasn't. "I haven't allowed myself to owe Hecate a debt in a millennium."

"I thought you were friends."

"Hecate does nothing for free." Cole snorted like the idea was ridiculous. "And yet, I'd have given her anything to turn you back. When I felt... saw you there. Skin gray. Expression terrified. Eyes pleading. I'd gladly damn that gorgon a hundred times over in vengeance."

It was hard to do anything other than stare at Cole. I... I meant something to him.

"I have actually had a dream of you," I said, voice unsteady. "Not the sparring kind. The kind you thought I meant."

"Tell me, little wolf." An order, but one I didn't fight.

"I dreamed of how you tasted. How you felt against me. Intimately. More than that." I forced the next words out. "Have you ever dreamed of me that way?"

"I've had a thousand waking dreams of you," Cole breathed.

And like that, the floodgates opened.

I barely had time to swallow my wine before we crashed against each other. The clatter of goblets was like fireworks.

I needed to focus. Needed to stay focused.

But moon, Cole made it impossible. The wine flavored our kiss. He demanded I let him in, and I obliged. His arms wrapped around me, a vise I didn't mind. My own hands moved, fisting his hair as if I could lock him against me.

This wasn't the kiss for dominance in the woods. No mistake, Cole was dominant, and I wasn't exactly submitting. But there was more. It was as tender as it was passionate. There was understanding. My body was alive under his, more than it ever had been before. His scent surrounded me and I never wanted to let go. I wanted to sink in his arms and never come up for air.

Mine, that possessive, primitive wolf in me thought. *Mine*.

Cole tried to break away to say something, but I continued the kiss, pressing my tongue against his. Tasting him. Wanting to be drunk. Wanting to sleep.

And then he collapsed.

I nearly fell with him, his arms wrapped around me, but I managed to disentangle myself. He slumped down involuntarily. His eyes were still open for a moment, fighting to stay awake as his mind caught up to what had happened.

Poison.

I had poisoned Cole with my kiss.

And the look in his eyes, the fury, the betrayal, said he knew what I had done.

And then his eyes shut.

I quickly swallowed the antidote I'd hidden in my clothes—a small handful of pomegranate seeds. Hecate had given me something that would stave off the worst of the effects from hitting me when taken in advance, but I couldn't cure myself until I'd taken the poison.

It was hard to look at Cole. Instinct urged me to check on him. He was so still, barely breathing. What if I'd really harmed him?

But what could I do? Wake him up? Cure him? Carry him to bed?

I had to trust I'd done it right and act fast. The book included a general description of the potion, but it offered little guidance on how long it would be in effect. I had to act fast.

I shook myself, willing the last of the sleepiness out of my body, and took off in the castle. It took me no time to find Cole's room—despite the fact I hadn't set foot inside it since that first day.

Hecate had, after much cajoling, given me the answers to getting back to the living realm. I'd known I needed a Libra demon, the kind that could make a portal. The only surefire way to find one was to go to the capital. And to get there, I needed a key, she'd said. A key Cole had in his room.

The room was unchanged from my memories, down to the same silk sheets he'd slept on. His scent covered the room, more than any other space. Guilt clawed at me, but I had no time. Daphne needed me. Hecate hadn't known where in the room I'd find it, but she'd described the key. A gem, white, polished, and glistening, the size of my palm. A moonstone, specifically.

I tore the room apart.

Panic spurred me on. Where I'd once been worried Cole might sleep forever, now I was motivated for fear he wouldn't sleep long enough. Did I have seconds? Minutes?

His dressers were the first. I ripped out each item, discarding it when no key fell out, and then started on the next. I flipped the mattress. Checked for loose stones in the wall. Moved furniture. I moved to the bathroom. The setup was similar to my own en suite, the sink. Identical to mine, but something was off.

Cole's room was luxurious but functional. Practical. His sink was set the same as mine, yet there was one addition. A decorative container of odd shaped soaps.

I reached in, feeling each oval in my hand. Discarding them once I felt the waxy texture. There's no way it's here. It's too cliche.

But then I felt it. Hard. Cold.

Stone.

A quick glance confirmed I'd found what I'd come for.

And with that, I took off. I nearly tripped on my own feet, running to the door. I ran faster than I ever had before, avoiding the kitchen.

As I raced out, I listened, expecting to hear his roar.

But no roar came.

And I was on my own again.

CHAPTER XXXIV

I SHIFTED TO MY wolf form once I crested the hill past the castle. It wasn't practical to stick to my human shape. I'd need to steal some clothes once I hit the capital, but that was the least of my problems. As for the moonstone, I carried it in my mouth.

As a wolf, the urge to return to Cole was stronger.

But the wolf part of me also understood this was for Daphne. I pushed away the feelings for Cole, the complicated tangle that ate at me.

I ran all night. It should've been hard to follow Hecate's directions, yet I found my way almost by instinct. It didn't make sense. But eventually, I scented water and found myself in front of the luminous lake I'd first been drawn to in the realm. Before, I'd simply thought the smell of the water was odd. Now, I realized that was because there was something more to the lake.

This had been the last of Hecate's instructions. Drop the moonstone into the water and I would soon find myself in the capital.

For a moment, there was nothing, nothing save the ripples in the water that soon faded.

Had I misunderstood? Or had Hecate lied?

But then, the water drained in front of me. Not the entire lake. No, it was as if the rest of the water remained untouched while the water directly in front drained further and further, forming steps. I hesitated only the barest second before taking the first step down, then quickly walked through the rest. The water dampened the fur of my paws, but nothing else. It made no sense, but so little did in this realm. By all rights, I was walking under the lake, but no water touched me anywhere else. If I looked up, I could see light shining through the water overhead. The path grew darker and darker, my shifter vision allowing me enough to see.

It wasn't a short journey, something Hecate could've stood to mention. Adrenaline and my preternatural stamina kept me going along the path for hours, but I was fatigued. Worried too. My plan had a lot of holes—how to find the demon, how to make it take me to the surface, how to even rescue Daphne. I hadn't exactly had a lot of time to lay out a plan.

One thing at a time.

I kept going down and down, and yet against any laws of physics, I eventually emerged from a cave. A glance down showed I was actually well above ground. Not too far in the distance, I saw what could only be the capital.

The city was lined with a tall wall around the perimeter,

but I could make out the tops of buildings. It was a dark city, no mistake, under the same red sky. Now, dawn had come. I'd been on the move all night.

My bones ached.

I leaped down the side of the mountain, balancing carefully. As I got lower, I saw more, smaller settlements on the fringes of the capital outside the wall. The farther out, the more sprawling.

A city.

It was bizarre. On the one hand, simply from the fact I'd only encountered a small handful of individuals since descending to this realm. But even in Moon-Ghost, our pack hadn't been more than a few hundred. We were considered large—Maddox often called us the largest pack in the continent, but I was suspicious of his tendency to self-aggrandize—but we weren't much more than a small town ourselves.

Ironic how many more things I was seeing dead compared to the vague life I'd lived before.

But the city was there. In sight.

Once I got there, the real work would begin.

Part of me wanted to push on at all costs. But the logical part, the one that had learned some form of restraint, cautioned me. I needed rest. Not a lot, but I was nearly dead on my paws as it was. Better to rest here. I didn't detect anyone nearby, scenting the air. I moved to a small inlet on the mountain, still slightly elevated and hidden from the ground but nowhere near as far up. I circled a few times to get comfortable, wrapped my russet tail around myself, and shut my eyes. *Just a few minutes,* I promised myself. *An hour at most.*

Sleep came quickly.

But I was not alone in it.

I was in darkness, but not the impossible darkness I sometimes found myself in. Rather than being in an utter void, it was more like I was in a room with the lights shut off, without the aid of my supernatural night vision. Like a human. Which, for a while, had been my status quo.

I wasn't in a room, though. I sensed I was outside. The feet beneath me were unsteady, the oxygen slightly thinned, like I was at an elevation. I knew it was a dream, in the way I always knew. They'd been sparse in the past months.

"There you are." The familiar disembodied voice. The one I'd heard in dreams for half a decade.

And then, the darkness eased just enough that I could make out another figure.

A massive, black wolf. Barely distinguishable from the dark.

I recognized him instantly. Cole.

The wolf spoke. "Little wolf, I'm coming for you."

The voice...

The voice was Cole's. Realization slammed into me. Impossible, inexplicable, yet undeniable.

The voice hadn't changed. Yet it was a perfect match for the one always in my dreams. I'd thought, on occasion, Cole's voice sounded familiar but had dismissed the thought each time. I could blame the fact I'd had only two—no, three—dreams in Hell. The one when I'd first arrived, before meeting Cole. The one where I'd been in a magical coma from Hecate's magic. And the third, when I'd been able to see Cole. Weeks apart.

But now, I could see it. I didn't understand how it was possible.

"It's been you all along." My voice wasn't more than a whisper.

His amber eyes glowed. "Tell me where you are."

I bared my teeth at the black wolf in front of me. Suddenly, I was a wolf, too. At least in my dream, though, I had some self-control.

"How can this be?" I felt like I was going insane. "You've known me all along."

"So, you finally recognize me."

"How have I dreamed of you before? Why didn't you say something?" This was another betrayal. Somehow, I knew it, even if I lacked the puzzle pieces. More secrets. I'd been played a fool.

"Answer my questions, Avery."

"No!" I roared. "You owe me an explanation."

Cole growled back, dominance rolling off him in waves. My fur stood on edge. But I wasn't backing down.

"This isn't the first time we've met, little wolf."

"You mean when I was in Moon-Ghost." How, how, how?

"No. Long before that."

I cast my mind back, flipping through memories like a Rolodex. The dreams, I now recalled. The first, before they'd been dark... I had seen him. Just once. It had been so long ago, and I'd told myself it was only a dream, but now I was certain.

I'd never seen Cole in a dream after that. He—who I'd thought was simply my subconscious—had been an incorporeal voice. He must have some type of control over the dreams.

"When?" I demanded.

Cole stalked closer.

"You heard Hecate call me the king."

I had. I had so many questions, so many Cole had refused to answer. Now that I had reached the capital, I had even more.

"Avery... You were once my queen."

He said the word with a gentle reverence I didn't think him capable of.

"No." The word was out of my jaws before I could even process what he meant. "You're screwing with me."

"I'll explain everything," Cole swore. "But don't go. I know what you're planning. There will be consequences, Avery. You can't know what you're about to unleash."

There would be consequences for Daphne if I didn't do this.

"You should've thought of that before you kept this from me," I snarled.

And then I forced myself out of the dreams vise and back into the waking world.

CHAPTER XXXV

I was in my human form once I woke up. I should've anticipated it.

Well, no sense shifting at this point. I could manage the last of the climb easily, and I'd need to communicate with whoever I came across anyway.

The knowledge that that dream had been more than a dream, that I'd really spoken to Cole, weighed on my bones. It was true. I couldn't begin to fathom what that would mean, but I didn't have time for that.

He'd asked where I was, yet said he knew what I was going to do. Translation: I might have some time, but not a lot.

I pushed all thoughts of Cole aside.

Daphne. I had to help Daphne.

I climbed down the last of the mountain. Once I looked up at it from the base, I better understood the scale. It was taller than I had initially thought. I set off for the city. I was only a few miles out. It was mostly open terrain, covered with tall grass. I stumbled on one of the small settlements I'd seen dispersed around the city, and I didn't waste the golden opportunity that an unguarded clothing line offered.

Add theft to my list of sins.

Well, what was going to happen? I was going to damn my soul to, um, Hell?

I tried to mark the place. Maybe one day I'd offer some reparations. But for now, I couldn't go around parading myself in the nude, even if shifters had more relaxed views of modesty.

To ease the guilt, I picked the most worn pieces of clothing. A simple pair of trousers, a loose-fitting shirt that would've fit Cole better than me, and a cloak that offered some protection from the slight chill of the atmosphere. I remained barefoot.

I eased out of the encampment quickly but wasn't able to resist tasting the different scents of the inhabitants. Not shifters. But some notes were familiar. The statues of all sorts of creatures had greatly expanded my understanding of the magical world, and I recognized some of those here.

Now dressed, I continued to the city. And it was a city. The walls I'd seen from a distance were solid stone, easily fifty feet tall. There was a ring outside the walls, but unlike Cole's moat of lava, there was only nothingness. I suspected if I dropped a stone to gauge the depth, it might be over a minute before I heard a sound.

The drawbridge was down, the gate open, saving me any trouble testing that theory.

I didn't know what I would tell any authority who stopped

me, but no one was around. For a capital city with big walls and a scary pit outside, they didn't seem too preoccupied with security.

The book I'd read had only given the vaguest details about Libra demons. The description had been abstract, talking about their "attention to detail" and "unnatural keenness for dealmaking." Height? Skin color? Number of eyes? A frickin' picture? Nope. Maybe if I'd had more time, I could've scoured the library for more books about demonology, but I'd perused most of the titles in the library at some point or another and come up empty.

The other two demons had been animalistic, one bull-headed, the other lion-bodied. But that went with their zodiac names. I tried to recall the symbol of the Libra but was coming up blank. I didn't think it was an animal one, though.

The inside of the city was unlike anything I expected. When you hear "capital of Hell" you picture pitchforks and brimstone. Of course, despite some unsavory characters, Hell also hadn't been as Hellish as I might've expected, if I'd known I would actually be going there.

The city was brimming with people. For my first few steps, I stumbled through, nearly open-mouthed as I marveled. People were moving around, calling out to each other. There was a market or something set up that looked fresh out of a medieval book. The snippets of haggling I listened in on said these weren't your usual fare—toad eyes and rat's breath rather than apples and pears—and the threats that went back and forth during the bargaining process were certainly, well, descriptive.

How big exactly is an ogre's toenail and how much would it hurt to have it shoved up there?

I'd never been around so many people. If I'd had time, I'd have been angry at Cole for denying me the ability to see this place before. I'd have explored at my leisure.

But I had to rescue Daphne.

Some wanderers noticed me. The hairs on my neck rose at the attention. A reminder this might be an interesting place, but I shouldn't linger. Shouldn't stand out or look like I didn't belong. I tugged my hood up closer to cover my red hair and continued on. The hair always drew attention—and contempt, when I'd been in the pack. I wandered through the throng of people, trying to figure out my next steps.

Tragically, there was no obvious sign declaring LIBRA DEMON HERE. I was going to need to ask someone. But who? Asking too many people might draw attention, and that seemed like a mistake waiting to happen. I zig-zagged up and down the aisles, keeping an ear out for anything that might help me. Bits of conversation about prices, flirting, a few brawls down alleyways. Different merchants called out, heralding their wares.

"Buy a bottle, get a bottle, real wishing well water!"

"Fresh potions! As powerful as Hecate's!"

"One bite of this and you'll be tupping like it's your last night alive!"

"Secrets, salacious and suspect, sold here…"

I turned towards the last one. It was the most promising I'd heard. I wove through the crowd. Different tents were set up, some barely taking up any space, while others were sturdy and basically functioned as shops. Most were single cart stands, sheltered under a makeshift tarp.

"Secrets, sold only once…" the voice said again. I honed in on the source.

It was a small tent on the fringe of the marketplace. I couldn't see the seller from outside. The tent was completely covered, having a split flap at the front.

I walked in.

And it was… empty? There was a small table, barely more than a side table, with a stool behind it. No one was on the stool, though.

"Seeking a secret?"

The voice had come from below. I glanced down, and there, on the floor, was a small cardboard box. And in the box… was a cat.

I frowned. I hadn't actually seen too many cats in MoonG-host. They didn't exactly get along with shifters, and shifters weren't the best pet owners. At least not in my pack.

Then again, this cat could talk, so obviously some rules didn't apply.

"I'm looking for someone. Can you help me find them?" I asked.

The cat hopped out of the box and arched, stretching. It had white fur, which was somehow clean despite the dirt floor, and pale blue eyes that were unnerving. In a bored voice, it informed me, "My trade is secrets, dog. I'm not a directory."

Crap. "Well, how to find them was kept secret from me. Does that count for anything?"

The cat hopped up on the stool and sat, looking at me. "Perhaps." The rumble of the r was a veritable purr. The cat might be playing it cool, but it did seem interested now. "Who are you seeking?"

"A Libra demon. One who can make a portal to another realm." I didn't want to reveal too much about which realm I was headed to. I shifted on my feet, waiting for an answer.

The cat lifted a paw and licked it, contemplating. The tarp of the tent effectively muffled all outside sounds, even from my enhanced hearing, leaving the wet sound as the only noise while the cat considered my request.

Me, I was trying to keep a straight face. This was serious, yes. But I was asking a cat for help finding a demon. Daphne would never believe this. I'd become pretty accepting of many oddities in Hell, but now that I was on my way back, well, it struck me how bizarre all this was.

"This is a secret I have," the cat said at last.

Thank the moon. "Great. Where do I find them?"

The cat hissed. The hiss turned to a hacking cough. The cat put two paws on the table and hacked and hacked. I was contemplating trying the Heimlich on the feline when it finally passed a hairball.

Ewwwwww.

I was so glad I wasn't a cat shifter.

"Not so fast, dog." The cat looked at me from over the hairball. "I don't give my wares for free."

"I don't have any money."

If a cat could snort, this one did. "I want nothing so ordinary as gold or jewels. I will give you this information. You must give me a secret in turn. One only you know."

A secret? "You first," I said.

The cat curled up on the stool and yawned.

Fine. Me first.I didn't exactly possess a certain other wolf's unending supply of secrets. "Um... I'm afraid of clowns." It was true. And it was embarrassing. I hadn't even told Daphne. The one time as children one of the adults had dressed up in face paint for one of the Alpha clique's birthday, I'd run all the way back home.

Home had been empty, even then.

"I can keep this information, if you prefer, dog. I offer you something of value, and I expect something valuable in turn."

I bit down on a growl. Plan B could be turning into a wolf and shaking the mangy thing in my mouth until it volunteered the information, but fair was fair. "I don't have any good secrets."

The cat's eyes seemed electric as it looked at me. "I doubt that. Tell me something no one else knows. Something you keep secret even to yourself. So secret, you don't even let yourself think it."

I opened my mouth and shut it. Something I kept secret from myself?

I racked my brain for an answer that would satisfy the cat. I needed an answer if I was going to save Daphne. I shut my eyes for a brief second, trying to put the complex swirl of emotions into words. I thought back, back before I was in Hell. To the time when I'd been in the pack.

And then, I had an answer. I didn't like it. The cat was right, I had kept it a secret from myself. Because I hadn't wanted to admit it. Acknowledge it.

I hated it. But I forced the words out anyway, because they were true.

"The night I found my moon-matched mate, the bond made me want him. Even though he'd tormented me for years. I know that now. But it wasn't just that, because he wasn't affected like I was. There was something else. And deep down, the reason I wanted him was because I thought if I mated with him, the pack would have to accept me. The torment would end. And in that brief moment, I was willing to ignore every cruel thing they'd ever done to me if it meant I'd finally be part of the pack. And when he killed me, and I knew I was dying without ever having had a place to belong, that was my last thought."

The cat looked at me for a long moment, a single, unimpressed blink its only reaction.

It's gonna be Plan B, isn't it?

But the cat sat up and jumped down from the stool, then walked over to me. It wove between my legs. "Satisfactory." Its tail trailed over my calves. "You will find your demon in the Lone Eye Tavern, three blocks west of here."

"How will I know who it is?"

The cat tensed, and I just knew it was about to go and lecture me on how that wasn't a secret and it wasn't its fault I didn't know. "Come on," I urged. "That was a juicy secret I gave you. Give me a freebie."

The cat made a sound that made me worry it was going to hurl up another hairball on my bare feet. "Very well. Libra demons can be identified by the tattoos that web over their skin. This one answers to the name Phaidros."

Okay. A real lead.

"Thank you." On a whim, I bent down and scratched the cat behind the ears. The cat gave a reluctant purr before returning to its cardboard box. I left the tent and wasted no time following the directions.

The tavern was thankfully easy to find, if only because it was loud and you could smell the booze a block away. I walked up to the door and was blocked by the... bouncer?

The creature was eight feet tall and had arms like tree trunks crossed over its chest. It looked down at me with its one eye and in a gravelly voice said, "No entry."

"I need to get in there," I said, refusing to be intimidated.

"Tavern is full." The giant took a menacing step forward.

I refused to be intimidated and take a step back. "I'll just be a minute."

"No."

"Yes," I countered eloquently. "I need to talk to someone in there. Let me pass."

The bouncer simply lifted its gaze and looked straight ahead, which was about three feet above where I was.

Oh, it's going to be like this?

No way was I letting this creature bully me out of my mission. "Let me pass," I repeated, trying to channel that menacing, dominant voice Cole had used so often. "I'm getting in there one way or another. I'd rather not hurt you."

It was a bit of a bluff, but I hoped he'd buy it.

By the roaring laughter that ensued, he did not.

I wasn't sure why the laughter set me off the way it did. Maybe it was the fact I'd been laughed at my entire life, for being weak, for being different, for not being able to defend myself. Maybe it was exhaustion that frayed my nerves, from everything I'd done to Cole and the fact I'd been on the run for almost an entire day. Maybe it was simple desperation, the knowledge that every minute I spent dealing with this asshole,

Daphne was suffering.

No matter what the reason was, I needed to get into the bar, and this burly oaf was blocking my way.

It wasn't like other times where I shifted because I lost control without realizing it from fear. No, this was anger that coursed through me. I unclasped my cloak, letting it sink to the ground, and launched myself at the cyclops.

Somehow, with his one giant eye, he missed the fact a wolf was about to attack him because he'd been too focused on acting like I didn't exist. His mistake. I clamped my jaws into one of those beefy arms.

He yelped, a high pitched sound that excited the predator in me.

Then he flung his arm into the tavern's front wall with me still hanging on by my jaws.

Ouch. But I didn't let myself feel the pain. I went for him again, this time diving low at the ankles. He tried to kick me off, but I'd already let go. As a wolf, I kept lower than his towering height. He was slow, too. He swung wildly at me but kept missing. Like with the Leo demon, I darted in and out. But my opponent didn't have the agility of that creature. He was strong, and if he got both hands around me, I was in real trouble. But I outpaced him.

Despite the strength of my jaws, I wasn't really making any progress. The cyclops didn't chase me when I darted away. He wasn't moving from his post at the door. I was a nuisance to him, but with his thick skin, he could withstand the worst of my bites and scratches.

I needed to do something else. Something he couldn't ignore.

I glanced around, snarling at the cyclops so he wouldn't realize I was gathering my thoughts. The street was mostly empty. But then, to the side of the tavern, there were some crates, maybe from a shipment of something.

I didn't see crates, though. I saw a launching pad.

Before the cyclops could react, I darted to the side and sprang up the boxes. I threw myself at the cyclops with all the force I could manage. He'd turned to follow the movement, a fatal flaw. His hands flew in front of his face and managed to snag my leg but not before I reached my target and scratched with my powerful claws.

Right in the eye.

He dropped me suddenly, and I had to roll aside to avoid him stumbling into me. I had no time for guilt. Instead, I quickly shifted back into my human shape and swiped my cloak and what remained of the tattered pants and put them on. The shirt was done for, but the cloak would cover me if I pinned it just right. Caring about modesty wasn't practical.

And if the Libra demon—Phaidros—was as friendly as the bouncer, I might be shedding the clothing again.

Whatever happened, I'd be ready.

I entered the bar.

CHAPTER XXXVI

T HE OVERWHELMING ALCOHOLIC SCENTS momentarily blinded my senses as I entered the bar. The space was effectively all made of wood and not the high-end stuff. Planks hastily nailed together made up tables and bar tops with barrels serving as stools. The place was packed. No one seemed to notice my entry. Then again, with all the noise and general intoxication, odds were they hadn't been able to hear the ruckus outside. Once the door closed behind me, I could barely make out the oaths the cyclops was bleating.

I scanned the inhabitants. The range of patrons was as varied as those at the marketplace, but while the individuals there had been powerful no doubt, they lacked the edge the creatures here had. It felt like any second a brawl could break out.

Creatures of every description were settled throughout. The bartender was the only one to take notice. She was fairly human-looking, except for the webbed fingers I noticed as she handed a mug to someone. There was a green-skinned, dwarven-looking creature playing cards with a woman so pale she could've been a ghost. When she flickered in and out before throwing her cards unhappily on the table, I realized she actually was one.

Others looked normal, but if I focused past the booze, I could tell there was more beneath the surface. But no other shifters.

I did a slow lap around the tavern, trying to find the Libra demon the secret-obsessed cat had assured me was here.

I'd nearly given up when there, in a shadowed corner at an almost-empty table, sat the male I'd been looking for. Unlike the other demons I'd met, he actually looked completely normal. Dark-skinned, symmetrical features, a build within an inch or so of Cole's, though where Cole was a warrior, this male looked like he was more suited for the life of a politician. In contrast to my tattered pants and cloak, he was in what nearly passed for a suit. Except it would've been a suit from maybe three hundred years ago with a jutted collar from the green jacket and poofy, storm-gray shirt sticking out.

But none of that was what signaled him as my target. No, it was the complex web of white that covered his exposed skin. Small dots, faint lines that seemed more like scars. They receded around his face, but I had no doubt that he was the demon. The air around him was heavy with the scent of cloves.

"I don't do that kind of sale, love," the demon said, not quite looking at me.

My cheeks flushed. I hadn't meant to stare, but I wasn't looking to approach people here willy-nilly. The male *was* attractive but in a too-pretty way. "Are you Phaidros?"

He slid his gaze over to me. "Depends who's asking."

I took that as confirmation and took a seat on the barrel stool across from him.

"By all means," he scoffed. "You should move along. Already had my fill of virgins for the week."

I gritted my teeth. "I need a portal, not a lay."

He lifted a hand and shooed me away, no longer looking at me. "Not in the mood to make portals, love."

I narrowed my gaze on the male. I didn't have to fake the threat of violence in my words. "I just maimed the guy outside the bar who tried to turn me away. I'm not really receptive to being shooed away tonight."

"Very scary," the male—Phaidros—said with a shrug. "In the interest of not being maimed, tell me. Where are you looking to portal to? Maybe a realm with cage fights to satisfy your thirst for maiming?"

"The realm of the living. Err, Moon-Ghost lands specifically."

Phaidros let out a low hum and steepled his fingers and tapped them on the table, not reacting.

"Can you do it?" I asked impatiently. "It's important."

"The question isn't if I can do it. I'm a Libra demon, and if you know enough to seek me out by name, then it should be beyond question. What I want to know is, what can you offer me?"

Yeah. There was the little hitch in my plan. One of a hundred. "I have nothing to bargain with," I admitted, slightly chagrined. "But—"

Phaidros turned away.

A low growl escaped my throat. I leaned forward, my hood falling back from the movement. "Listen—"

The movement caught his attention, and the male turned back to face me, a refusal already on his lips.

But something changed. He looked at me again, as if seeing me for the first time. His gaze went first to my hair, then back to my face.

"I'll take a favor," the demon declared.

I blinked, taken aback by his sudden agreement. "What kind of favor?"

"Does it matter?" he replied congenially. "You'll agree, anyway."

Well, he had me there. And I really didn't have anything to offer except a meaningless favor. It was unlikely I'd see the demon again. "Fine. When can we leave?"

"Right after you say these words." He scribbled something on a scrap of parchment and slid it over to me.

The words seemed like nonsense, but I had no other choice. "I swear to the Styx I will pay back this favor. Now, when can we leave?" I repeated.

Phaidros lifted himself from his seat. I stood as well, though the male towered over me. "No time like the present."

I wasn't sure what answer I'd been expecting, but I wasn't about to complain. Every minute I delayed meant another Daphne suffered. Phaidros asked a few more details as to where exactly I wanted to be "dropped off" and I gave them, still shocked that this was happening. I was going back. It was really happening.

The Libra demon wasted no time making the portal. He turned towards the wall to his left in that shadowy corner and rubbed his palms together. A minute later, he pressed his palms up against the wall, then split them as they went down opposite sides before rejoining at the bottom. It was hardly the ceremony I'd expected, but then again, Hecate could transform her entire garden with the flick of a wrist, and I suspected that was mainly theatrics.

And just like that, there was a portal. It had a slight yellow glow, sparks flickering throughout, but through it, I could see the exact, familiar terrain I'd left behind.

"If you're waiting for an engraved invitation, that wasn't covered in our bargain," Phaidros said in a bored voice.

I shoved past the demon, not hesitating another second before jumping through.

Time to rescue my friend.

Epilogue

T O SAY THE ROOM was in disarray would be an understatement.

Some of it, no doubt, had been from the girl searching for the stone. Honestly, Hecate could've thought of a hundred better hiding spots, but he had never been known for his creativity. Not in this arena, anyway. The male was a god of many things, yet a rank novice at deception.

Hecate regarded him from the edge of the space. He was protective of his bedroom, and with his current ire, she had no desire to push on that particular nerve.

But the rest of the destruction was due solely to him.

Stones were missing from the wall. The bed was in splinters. Sheets and clothes torn asunder.

All told, it was rather impressive, considering the castle was long since enchanted to be self-maintaining.

He heaved, sweat-soaked from exertion, as well as the after-effects of the potion. Hecate didn't know exactly how the girl had managed to get him to ingest the powder, but whatever way, he'd received a potent dose. It might well have knocked a lesser creature down permanently or for at least a year. He'd shaken the worst of it off in hours, but it made no difference. The moonstone, and the girl, were gone.

If he was tired, perhaps he could finally talk rather than roar like an animal.

In fairness, a lot of the roaring was directed at Hecate herself.

"Are you ready to be reasonable yet?" Hecate called from the doorway.

Furious eyes turned on her, as if finally noticing her. Despite the fact he'd summoned her the moment he'd awoken.

It was unfair to accuse her. The girl was clever enough to have managed the entire thing on her own, and truly, Hecate had only offered the barest assistance.

"You're responsible for this." His voice was pure menace.

Only through the least complicated lens. "I'd say the responsibility is yours, my king."

"How do you figure?" It was phrased as a question, but it was a threat. Violence rolled off the male in waves, promising vengeance if only he could find the right target. Even in all his fury, though, Hecate didn't expect he'd actually strike at her.

Probably.

If they did tangle, the realm would suffer the aftereffects. In her vanity, she imagined she'd hold her own, but her king had been separated from that female, and that made him... unpredictable. Unpredictable, the same way the room was merely in disarray.

But it did no good to show him a browbeaten servant. Hecate cocked a hand to her hip. "You can't keep her on a leash. It was going to snap sooner or later."

"A leash? I was keeping her safe, something you were all too quick to undo. I never should have let her train with you."

"I'll remind you, you brought her to me because she turned into stone under *your* care." She didn't dare mention how close Soteria had been to being beyond saving. "That overgrown snake should've been pruned eons ago, and you had no right to deny her the ability to develop her skills."

The animalistic growl from him said he was unpersuaded.

Hecate gentled her voice. "She is resourceful. All is not lost." Not again. She knew that protectiveness was born out of past failures. But to her view, they were not the failures her king still blamed himself for.

"You should have told her no! You should've come directly to me, not supplied her with the damn poison."

"Oh, no, the poison was all hers," Hecate assured him.

"Damn you, witch!" There went another piece of furniture at the wall. It had been such a nice end table.

"Truly. What would you have had me do? You expected me to deny her? She, who is my queen and yours?"

At that, he finally stilled.

"No," Hades at last agreed. "But you will aid me in getting her back. Consequences be damned."

And consequences... there would be many.

Thank you for reading Forsaken Mate! If you sign up for my newsletter hereor at VasilisaDrakeBooks.com, you can read about the first time Cole and Avery *really* met... And if you're dying from that cliffhanger, be sure to pick up *Forgotten Queen*!

Acknowledgments

This book has been a journey like no other. Forsaken Mate started out as a little "happiness project" I worked on in between other projects and my own work. I published on a platform called Kindle Vella. Some of you found me there and followed me to this book (hello!) and I'm so grateful, because seeing people eagerly devouring the updates every week gave me the motivation to keep going. A special thank you goes out to every single person who took a chance on me there.

Thank you to the BookTok community for embracing this book and making this publication even possible.

Thank you to Magan (Court of Spice Editing Services) and PollyAné (Proofs by Polly) for editing my messy manuscript. This book would have been impossible without you both.

Thank you to Christian (Covers by Christian) for designing a cover I love more than I ever could have imagined.

Thank you to Z for creating my first ever fantasy map.

Thank you to my friends and family for supporting me in this process, and to the writing communities I've been lucky enough to find companionship and support while bringing this book to life.

Writing Forsaken Mate was also a journey unlike any other because it's not done yet. I'm used to typing "The End" and shutting the book, but if you're here, you know we still have a lot to do. So, most of all, I want to thank you, dear reader, for taking a chance on this book and I hope to see you next time in Forgotten Queen.

ABOUT THE AUTHOR

Vasilisa Drake is based in New England and is constantly bouncing from city to city while she tries to find her home amidst overpriced rental apartments. Forsaken Mate is Vasilisa Drake's debut, though she's written contemporary romance under another name for several years. Fantasy romance is her first love, closely followed by pet dragons and men who are obsessed with their women. She can be found staying up way too late reading, organizing her bookshelf for the millionth time, and winning the imaginary arguments in her head at least 30% of the time.

She can be contacted via email at VasilisaDrakeBooks@gmail.com or on TikTok @VasilisaDrakeBooks

Find Vasilisa

You can find Vasilisa on several platforms including:

Bookbub

Goodreads

Romance.io

Storygraph

TikTok